Praise for the Black Falcon Trilogy

"A multilayered, complex plot with lushly evocative prose and darkly erotic passages."

—*Booklist* on *It Wakes in Me*

"This dramatic and involving story will transport readers to another time, where women were the power players in society. The historical detail and vivid descriptions make this a fascinating and compelling read."

—*Romantic Times BOOKreviews* on *It Wakes in Me*

"Kathleen O'Neal Gear has brought alive, with extraordinary vividness and realism, the lives of the first Americans in her splendid novel *It Wakes in Me*. I read this dramatic and haunting novel in one sitting. Gear is more effective than any time machine in transporting the reader back to the vast, beautiful, and unspoiled world of prehistoric North America."

—Douglas Preston, *New York Times* bestselling author of *Tyrannosaur Canyon*

"Vivid . . . Gear provides plenty of intrigue . . . and spices things up now and then with steamy, erotic passages."

—*Kirkus Reviews* on *It Wakes in Me*

"A well-written tragedy. Captures the culture of these people."
—*The Romance Readers Connection* on *It Dreams in Me*

"A highly textured piece of writing . . . The reader can literally feel the panic rising within the nations as they fight for control." —*Fallen Angel Reviews* on *It Dreams in Me*

IT DREAMS IN ME

KATHLEEN O'NEAL GEAR

A TOM DOHERTY ASSOCIATES BOOK
NEW YORK

This is a work of fiction. All of the characters, organizations, and events portrayed in this novel are either products of the author's imagination or are used fictitiously.

IT DREAMS IN ME

Copyright © 2007 by Kathleen O'Neal Gear

Map and chapter ornaments by Ellisa Mitchell

A Forge Book
Published by Tom Doherty Associates, LLC
175 Fifth Avenue
New York, NY 10010

www.tor-forge.com

Forge® is a registered trademark of Tom Doherty Associates, LLC.

ISBN-13: 978-0-7653-5024-4
ISBN-10: 0-7653-5024-6

First Edition: June 2007
First Mass Market Edition: August 2008

Printed in the United States of America

0 9 8 7 6 5 4 3 2 1

IT DREAMS IN ME

HE IS AFRAID.

I know because he trembles when I press my naked body against his and whisper, "You were a fool to come back here."

His wide eyes are sheathed with the amber glitter of sparks that suffuse the smoke. The only article of clothing he wears is a bright red sash wrapped around his throat. His beautiful cape, made from woven buffalo wool, rests two paces away with his other belongings: his bow and quiver, his gorgeous coral-inlaid war club, deer-bone stiletto, and copper jewelry.

"What do you want!" He strains against the ropes that bind his hands and ankles. "Why are you doing this?"

"You can't be that stupid. You must know who sent me."

The dark forest has gone deathly quiet. The only sounds are the falling rain and the occasional crackling of timbers that rise from the smoldering heaps of lodges in the distance.

He tries to speak. His mouth opens, but no words come out, just a strange hiss, like the last breath leaving a dying body.

Finally he says, "I did what she asked! Go back and tell her I obeyed her. I obeyed even though I knew it was the wrong thing to do!"

I smile.

His jaw trembles before he clenches his teeth.

I stare down into his eyes, and pure terror stares back. He is a powerful man, muscular, brown, with deep lines across his forehead; he is one of the great leaders of the Water Hickory Clan . . . was one of the great leaders.

Ten paces away a little boy lying in a pool of rain-diluted blood kicks and goes limp, still clutching his make-believe bow in his hand.

"I don't believe you," he hisses. "She wouldn't do this. I am her loyal servant! She knows that!"

Against his lips, I murmur, "Don't be afraid."

He forces a hard swallow down his throat. "What are you going to do to me?"

I reach down to stroke his limp manhood, and his eyes change; disbelief vies with hope. I have a reputation for being a passionate woman, and it has occurred to him that perhaps this is an erotic game, that I ambushed him, clubbed him senseless, and tied him up to pleasure him at my will. Within moments he is rigid in my hand.

"Don't be afraid," I repeat as I slip his manhood inside me.

He can't stop himself; he tries to force himself deeper, but his bound hands and legs make his movements awkward.

I spread my legs to help him. As I lazily rock against him, his eyes gleam. Fear has excited him in a way he's never experienced before. He likes this game and drives himself into my soft sheath.

When he's panting and writhing, I lean forward, dragging my breasts across his bloody chest, and say, "I'm going to set your souls free."

In the midst of his euphoria, uncertainty clouds his gaze. But it is brief. He's close. He cares about nothing but finishing.

I grasp the sash around his throat and sit up. Every time he thrusts, I twist the sash, tightening it. I smile at him with my lips open, and he thinks he understands. As he nears completion, suffocation heightens the sensations in a desperate fashion. He struggles for air and senselessly lunges against me. The smile on his face is sublime.

By the time his seed jets in a warm ancient rhythm, he's wheezing, gasping for air.

When he finally relaxes and dreamily stares up at me, he sees himself reflected in my eyes.

And he knows.

"No!" He slams his head into my chest, knocking

me backward to the wet ground. I lose my grip on the sash, and hideous grunts escape his throat as he tries to crawl away, flopping and rolling, moving like the worm he is.

I stride forward, grab the trailing ends of the sash, and drag him toward the marsh, where the cattails have begun to gleam faintly blue in the dawn light penetrating the clouds. Deadfall cracks beneath his flailing feet.

While he twists and grunts, I study the dark dots of birds perched on the marsh reeds. The coppery scent of blood mixes with the fragrance of wet earth as though they were born together and have never been separate.

At the edge of the water, I stop. Chief Short Tail's face has turned purple, and his mouth opens and closes like a fish's.

I loosen the sash.

When he begins to gasp, I kneel down and stare into his disbelieving eyes. "This is going to take time, Chief. Get as much air as you can. Scream if you need to. Your warriors are out tracking down the survivors of the massacre. There's no one to hear you.

"No one but me."

A RATTLE SOUNDED TO RED RAVEN'S LEFT. HE scanned the towering oaks. Birds and squirrels perched in the branches, frozen in place, silent, as though they, too, had heard the sound of human feet. Far off, but coming fast.

The glow of dawn penetrated the misty rain, but most of the world remained in deep shadow.

All night long terrified people had run past his hiding place, some dragging crying children by the hands, others, the lucky ones, carrying injured loved ones.

A thump, closer . . .

He held his breath.

Rain dripped through the branches and poured down upon the old leaf mat, creating a cadence that resembled a soft drumroll.

Rain. Just rain. Not footsteps.

He eased forward again, pushing aside the dark curtains of hanging moss while he tried to see through the storm. The scent of smoke grew stronger.

"That old woman is going to get me killed," he whispered.

It wasn't Red Raven's fault that he'd arrived while the attack was in progress. How could he have known that Chief Short Tail would strike at night? Most men would have attacked at dawn, so they could see who they were killing. Because of Short Tail's brazen strategy, Red Raven had probably missed his chance to carry out his clan matron's orders.

A twig snapped.

He went rigid, then cursed himself when a squirrel darted by. For over a hand of time, he'd been jumping at every sound.

If he had any true courage he'd just go home, tell old Sea Grass that he hadn't seen either of the people she'd sent him to find, and face her wrath. But these things had to be handled with great care. While circumstances might prevent a man from carrying out his clan matron's orders, if it was discovered that he'd deliberately disobeyed her, his life would be worth less than a squirrel skin. Still, it was too dangerous to remain here. Survivors roamed the woods, waiting until they knew it was safe to come back and bury their dead relatives. Any member of the Water Hickory Clan that they found alive would wish he were dead.

Red Raven took another step. . . .

Ten paces away, the dark form of a woman moved through the forest. Tall, with full breasts and swinging hips, she walked with a purpose. Her waist-length black hair stuck wetly to her back.

Red Raven drew his war club, parted the moss, and veered around underbrush, paralleling the woman's course. She went to a rotted log at the edge of the marsh and sank down as though weary. In front of her, dropped belongings lay strewn, kicked about in panic by people fleeing the attack.

"He's dead. I want you to know that," she said.

Red Raven frowned. Was she speaking with the lost ghosts who wandered the burned village? Or the dead Water Hickory Clan warriors who lay before her?

I should kill her. . . .

A man emerged from the trees and Red Raven dodged behind the curtain of hanging moss.

The man's wide surprised eyes gleamed in the storm light. He called, "What are you doing here? I told you I'd take care of it!"

"You took too long; besides, it was my duty, not yours." She reached down and pulled a cape from the ground. As she swung it around her shoulders, she said, "He was such a fool. No true warrior would have been careless enough to allow me to catch him." She tied the cape laces beneath her chin. "Now let's go before his warriors come. They're already looking for him."

The man's gaze focused on what appeared to be a black pile leaning against an oak trunk. "Dear gods, what have you done?"

"He defied our matron. He deserved more than just death," she said, and walked away, heading up the deer trail into the trees.

The man ran to the pile and flipped over what was clearly a dead body.

Curious, Red Raven edged closer. He thought he recognized the man's voice, but couldn't be sure; he wasn't going to take the chance of calling out and having an enemy's arrow lodge in his chest.

The man examined the corpse, and his mouth set in a grim expression. He leaned down and said, "Fool! Now who will . . . our clan matron . . . I received . . . message."

The man turned and sprinted away, following the same trail the woman had taken.

Hallowed Ancestors, did he say "our" clan matron?

Red Raven tiptoed through the brush until he could see the corpse. The victim was naked, and he'd been strangled. His eyes and tongue still bulged from his skull. More than that, he had something, a sash maybe, tied around his throat.

Red Raven squinted. Copper glittered near the body. He moved closer. The objects, mostly jewelry, had been arranged around the corpse in a big circle. A mound of weapons and wadded clothing marked the center of the circle, and it occurred to Red Raven that they must have spilled from the dead man's back when the stranger flipped him over.

A sudden chill went up Red Raven's spine. This man's death was not the result of one warrior pitted against another in the heat of battle, but murder. The woman had been sending a message to anyone who found the body.

He frowned at the circle. If it had been made from colored sand instead of copper jewelry it would have resembled a Healing Circle.

That struck him as too bizarre to believe. Who would murder a man, then create a Healing Circle around him to protect his souls from evil Spirits?

Red Raven glanced around to make certain he was alone before he crept close to the body.

Had there been anyone near, his sudden intake of breath would have been his doom. He couldn't take his eyes from the coral-inlaid war club.

It was Short Tail's club and had been the chief's most cherished weapon. He'd made it himself and boasted that the gods had blessed it. Everyone knew that club.

Red Raven stood in shock until it occurred to him that that club might be his salvation. He couldn't have delivered Matron Sea Grass' message when Short Tail was already dead. Here was the proof! Chief Short Tail would never let that club out of his hands short of death.

She will still punish me for failing to deliver her

second message, but I'll just tell her that I saw no one else.

When he stepped into the ritual circle to pick up the club, a soft moan escaped the corpse's mouth. Red Raven almost screamed. He grabbed the club, leaped out of the circle, and ran a few paces before he looked back.

"He can't be alive!"

Shaking like a twelve-winters-old boy on his first war walk, Red Raven had to clench his teeth to steady his nerves.

The sash around Short Tail's throat must have loosened when he'd been flipped over, and this was air finally escaping his lungs.

That's even worse!

Terror warmed his veins.

The Black Falcon Nation believed that each person had three souls: a soul that lived in the eyes, a soul that lived in the shadow, and a soul that lived in the reflection. One of the Black Falcon People's greatest fears was that they might catch a dying person's last breath. It was at that moment that the reflection-soul and shadow-soul slipped out together. If a living person was too close to the breath, the shadow-soul, desperately looking for a new home, could shoot like an arrow into the living person, where it might nest for many winters.

The shadow-soul was terrifying because at death all the evil leached from the other souls and settled in the shadow-soul. That left the reflection-soul pure, fit to live among the Blessed Ancestors, while the cleansed eye-soul stayed with the body forever.

"I was too far away for his shadow-soul to reach me, wasn't I?"

He clutched the club and ran for Blackbird Town as fast as his legs would carry him.

THUNDERBIRDS RUMBLED ACROSS THE SKY, AND lightning flashed through her dreams like a war lance.

Chieftess Sora woke with a start. Tears ran down her cheeks as the last of the nightmare faded.

She looked up and blinked at the palm-thatch ramada that sheltered her. The four poles and roof had been hastily thrown up, for there were gaps in the fronds that allowed the rain to penetrate. Drops beaded the foot of the buffalohide that covered her.

She felt weak and bewildered. Where was she? She didn't recognize this place.

Cool wind eddied through the cypress trees, scenting the world with a pleasant tangy fragrance. She inhaled, hoping it would ease her nausea . . . while she tried to remember the past few days. Images flitted, bare scraps of horror filled with the scent of blood.

Her stomach heaved. She rolled to her side and vomited onto the ground.

Brush thrashed in the forest as someone trotted up the trail. Priest Strongheart emerged into the small clearing and hurried toward her with his long deerhide cape flapping around his legs. He had seen twenty-three winters, nine winters less than she had. Tall and skinny, he had short black hair. He was a homely man, his round face too wide, hooked nose too long, but his luminous eyes seemed to contain all the light in the world.

"Please, lie down," he called as he gracefully walked toward her. "You haven't eaten in two days. If you rise too fast, you'll be even sicker."

He picked up a flat piece of bark, scooped up the vomit, and tossed it out into the rainy forest; then he knelt at her side. His large calloused hand felt cool when he placed it against her forehead. "You're still hot, but much cooler than last night. Let me get you a cup of tea."

"Have I been ill?"

"Your reflection-soul has been out wandering for at least three days."

It was the reflection-soul that traveled to the afterlife at death. But sometimes, while a person was still alive, it wandered away from the body and became lost in the forest. That's what caused insanity. It took a very great Healer to find the lost soul and make it stay in the body.

She watched him walk over to the fire pit sheltered by the moss-covered branches of an old oak. Hanging from a tripod at the edge of the flames, a tea pot swayed in the wind. The misty background highlighted the shape of his tall body. He had broad shoulders that narrowed to a slim waist. Yellow starbursts decorated his buckskin cape.

Strongheart dipped two wooden cups into the pot and brought them back. "Drink this. You'll feel better."

She propped herself on one elbow and took the cup. The pungent fragrance of magnolia bark bathed her face as she sipped it. "Where are we?"

"Near Blue Heron Swamp," he answered, and blew on his tea to cool it.

"What—what happened?"

He stared at her as though he could see straight to the darkest depths of her souls. "I'm not sure. I went out into the forest to hunt, and when I returned Flint told me you were gone, that you'd slipped away from him. I said I would search the trails heading north; he searched the southern trails."

"Who found me?"

"Flint did. He said you had gone back to Eagle Flute Village. We brought you here as quickly as we could, and then Flint left. He told me he'd return soon, but it's been two days."

"Where did he go?"

"I don't know."

She drank the tea one sip at a time. His concerned gaze never left her. He seemed to be examining every bruise on her face and scratch on her arms.

Worriedly, he asked, "Are you better?"

A strange feeling gripped her, as though someone had reached inside her chest and squeezed her heart. "I had a nightmare."

"About what?"

She took another drink of tea to steady her nerves. "The same one. I've told you about it before."

He knelt beside her. "The dream about Flint and the Red Hill?"

"Yes, I—I don't have it as often as I used to. Only on rainy nights. And even then, over the past quarter moon, it's lost some of its reality. Now, when the dream comes, I usually know that the pain in my belly is not poison. I can tell myself that it's the wind I hear, not Flint singing me lullabies. And . . ." A deep soul-wrenching ache swelled her chest. "My souls don't rip apart when that tiny blue boy is born."

He reached out and brushed the black hair away from her eyes, then tipped her chin up to force her to look at him. His luminous eyes bulged slightly. "It wasn't your fault. I've told you that before, but you still don't believe me, do you? That's why your shadow-soul keeps walking backward in time to relive that event."

She fumbled with her tea cup. "I can't help it. My—my son is growing up inside me. Every night he gets a little older. Every morning I grieve his death."

Though she had been faithfully married to Flint for fourteen winters, he'd been afraid she was pregnant with another man's child. She wasn't. But he hadn't believed her. He'd wanted to kill the baby and make certain she could never have another man's child. The poison he'd given her had worked better than he'd planned. It had killed her ability to have anyone's child. At least, no man's seed had planted in her womb since that day.

Strongheart shifted to sit cross-legged on the edge of her buffalohide. "Do you recall anything from the past few days?"

"Just images. Things that make no sense."

"What things?"

She closed her eyes and watched them again. "Screaming children running through the forest . . . houses burning . . . a—a dead man propped against a tree."

His expression slackened, but he said nothing.

"What is it?" she asked. "Do the images mean something?" *Blessed gods, what have I done this time?*

"Do you recall that Eagle Flute Village was attacked?"

Her hand trembled; she had to set her cup down.

Several days ago Flint had taken her to Eagle Flute Village hoping that Strongheart could Heal her. She suffered from the Rainbow Black, an illness that caused people to see rainbows just before they fell down jerking all over.

"I don't recall anything," she answered. "What happened? Who attacked?"

Strongheart reached out to gently touch her hand. "I'm sorry. I shouldn't have told you so soon. You just awakened."

"I was once the high chieftess of the Black Falcon Nation. I *must* know what's happening out there. Who attacked your village?"

"Flint tells me they were members of his clan, the Water Hickory Clan."

She gave him a searching look. "Did your village fight back?"

"The Water Hickory warriors attacked at night. Many of our people were in their blankets. Some escaped, but not many."

"Your family?"

He bowed his head and for a long time just stared at the wet ground. "Several were killed."

Lightning flashed overheard, and Strongheart's hooked nose cast a curved shadow on his cheek. He was making an effort to keep his voice even, but she heard the pain just beneath the surface.

She said, "This is my fault. If I'd been in Blackbird Town, I would have found a way to stop it."

Blackbird Town was the capital of the Black Falcon Nation. Their leader, High Matron Wink, was her oldest and most cherished friend.

Strongheart looked up. "You think that the other clans knew about the attack, then?"

"I don't know, Strongheart." She ran a hand through her tangled hair. "I don't know."

"Perhaps it's best not to assume you could have stopped it," he said in a kind voice. "At least until we know what really happened."

"You once told me that guilt was fear, that it was my

way of punishing myself for being afraid. I think I finally understand what you meant."

"Do you?"

"Yes. I'm afraid that my best friend, Wink, needs me desperately . . . and instead I'm here with you." Angry tears burned her eyes. She blinked them away. "I'm here wasting your time."

He finished his tea and got to his feet. "Are you telling me you don't believe you can be Healed? Or you think I'm too poor a Healer to accomplish the task?"

She clenched her fists and in frustration shouted, "I'm too broken to be Healed! Can't you see that? Let me go home where I can be of some use!"

As he walked back toward the fire pit, he asked, "Are you hungry? There's some duck soup left over from breakfast."

She didn't answer. She felt shattered, certain that no one would ever be able to fix her wandering reflection-soul in her body. Finally, she responded, "I might be able to keep down some broth."

He dipped a cup into the pot sitting at the edge of the coals and walked back. As he handed it to her, he said, "You realize, don't you, that if you go home before you're Healed, you will probably be killed by your own people?"

She clamped her jaw to keep it from trembling.

The illness that Strongheart called the Rainbow Black took a strange form inside her. Sora had seen it. It was a dark wicked spirit, a *Midnight Fox*. Flint believed that her reflection-soul wandered away, roaming the forest while her body committed murder. If Strongheart couldn't find her lost soul and make it stay in her body, her clan would have no choice but to protect itself.

Gently, he pointed out, "If the Midnight Fox seizes you again and someone—anyone—in the village dies, you will be blamed."

Blamed and killed for it. Not even Wink would be able to save her, not this time.

As her throat tightened and tears burned her eyes, she set her bowl down.

Strongheart smoothed her hair. "Eat. Then get some sleep. We'll be moving again soon. You will need your strength."

VOICES PENETRATED AROUND THE DOOR CURTAIN
to the council chamber in the Matron's House at Blackbird Town.

For a few moments, High Matron Wink stood in the
dim hallway, listening to the three men inside the chamber. She couldn't make out any of their words, but their
indignant tones told her a great deal.

She straightened the conch shell combs that pinned
her graying black hair behind her ears and smoothed
the wrinkles from her purple dress. She had seen
thirty-six winters and felt every one today. Weariness
draped her body like an iron cape. As she ducked beneath the door curtain into the torchlit council chamber, the three men rose to their feet.

The council chamber was twenty paces across, and
sacred masks lined the walls, divine beings that watched

over the Black Falcon People. Birdman, Sun Mother, and the different Comet People were her favorites. Their empty eye sockets seemed to be staring straight at her. As she walked by, the streaming hair of the Comet People swayed and the scent of long-dried herbs filled the air.

Four log benches framed the fire hearth. When she neared them, the men bowed.

Her sixteen-winters-old son, Chief Long Fin, stood directly in front of her. He looked regal today. His golden cape fell around his tall body like sculpted sunlight. One long black braid hung down his back. To his left stood War Chief Feather Dancer, a heavily scarred man with a thumblike nose; to his right was a short man with hunched shoulders. He had small shining eyes and a twitching nose that reminded Wink of a trapped packrat. *Red Raven.* Matron Sea Grass' secret messenger. Every time she had a task too onerous for a decent person to complete, she paid this snake to do it. While Wink had never met him, she had several allies in the Water Hickory Clan who'd been watching him for winters.

"Please sit down," she said as she walked to the one open bench and sank down atop it. "We have a good deal to discuss. I assume you are Red Raven?"

The little man swallowed hard. "I am, High Matron. I was surprised when you sent War Chief Feather Dancer to drag me out of my chamber. May I ask why I have been summoned?"

The pearls on the sleeves of her long purple dress

shimmered when she reached for one of the cups resting beside the tea pot and dipped it full. The fragrances of bumblebee honey and dried palm berries wafted up with the steam.

For ten heartbeats, she sipped her tea and studied the men. Long Fin grimaced as though he, too, was upset by being ordered to appear in her council chamber at such short notice. Feather Dancer, on the other hand, glared so steadily at Red Raven that the man couldn't sit still. He kept shifting on his bench.

Wink set her cup aside and said, "I understand that you are the man who found Chief Short Tail."

Red Raven's eyes darted around the chamber before coming back to her. "How do you know about that?"

"Did you or didn't you?"

Feather Dancer drew his war club from his belt and placed it across his lap.

"High Matron, please," Red Raven said without taking his eyes from Feather Dancer. "I was on a personal mission for my clan matron. I'm sure she would not wish me to discuss the details—"

"Rumor has it that you saw a woman in the forest just before you discovered his body. Is that true?"

Red Raven's jaw clenched. He seemed to be assessing the situation, wondering how she knew this information. He must know he couldn't get away before Feather Dancer smashed his skull, and even if he did, she would order him hauled back and held under guard until he answered her questions . . . or disappeared never to be seen again.

"I have also heard that there was a man who came to get her. Are these things true?"

"I don't know what you're talking about!"

Wink got to her feet. "Three days ago, Water Hickory Clan went against the Council of Elders and attacked a Loon village, Eagle Flute Village. It was treason. Because the council wished to avoid civil war, it voted not to throw Water Hickory Clan out of the Black Falcon Nation, but we will be reassessing that decision at dusk today. Your clan's position is very tenuous. *Your* position is even more tenuous. Do you understand me?"

"But I am just a humble messenger, High Matron!"

She turned to Feather Dancer. "War Chief, I must go and prepare myself for the council meeting. I'll be occupied for the rest of the day. In my absence, please convince Red Raven that his cooperation is necessary."

"Yes, Matron." Feather Dancer gripped his war club and walked around the fire to loom over Red Raven.

Long Fin paled as though he found his mother's methods distasteful. He knew so little about the way the world worked. She blamed herself. All of his life, she'd sheltered and coddled him.

Boldly, Long Fin said, "Mother, as high chief I must tell you that I don't like—"

She turned her back on him and strode for the door.

Just as she gripped the curtain and pulled it aside, Red Raven called, "Well, maybe I—I do recall some of those things."

Wink looked back over her shoulder. "For your sake, I hope you recall all of them."

He looked up into Feather Dancer's scarred face and, in a very conciliatory voice, replied, "I would take it as a great favor, High Matron, if you gave me your oath that no one will ever know I spoke with you tonight."

She nodded.

He heaved a sigh and said, "Very well."

She marched back across the chamber and seated herself to his left. "Go on."

Feather Dancer didn't move. He continued standing beside Red Raven with his war club in his hand.

Red Raven glanced up at him before saying, "Five days ago, Matron Sea Grass sent me off with a message for Chief Short Tail. I was supposed to find him before the attack on Eagle Flute Village, but instead of waiting for dawn, as she'd ordered him to, the fool attacked at night." He ran a sweating hand through his black hair. "I had to hide until the battle was done. And it wasn't easy! Enemy warriors swarmed all around me. Were it not for my courage—"

"Tell me about the woman."

His lips pursed, unhappy that he hadn't been able to regale her with stories of his bravery. He said, "I saw her long after the battle was over. She walked through the forest, sat down on a log, and looked out at the smoldering village. She said, 'He's dead. I want you to know that.' I don't know what she meant. She seemed to be staring down at two dead Water Hickory warriors."

"What did she look like?"

He gestured uncertainly. "Tall, with long black hair. It was dark; I couldn't see very well."

"What was she wearing?"

"Nothing."

Wink paused, absorbing that. "Then what happened?"

"I was thinking about killing her when a man ran out of the forest, gasped at the sight of her, and said, 'What are you doing here?' Then she said something like, 'He was a fool. He defied our matron.'"

"Did you recognize her?"

"No. But, as I said, it was dark."

"What about her voice—had you heard it before?"

Red Raven tilted his head. "Now that you mention it, there was something familiar about it, but I didn't recognize it."

Hope reared like a wild animal inside Wink. Sora had been her best friend for twenty-five winters. Since the attack on Eagle Flute Village she had been desperate to know if Sora was alive or dead. She'd sent search parties out to comb the forests. She'd even hired a woman to pick through the ruins of Eagle Flute Village for any sign of Sora's body. They'd found nothing.

The woman Red Raven saw might have been Sora. It sounds like Sora.

"What did the man do after she left?"

Red Raven shrugged. "He went over to Short Tail's body—though, at the time, I didn't know it was Short

Tail's body—flipped him over, and said, 'You fool, now who will tell our clan matron that I received her message?' "

"What message?"

"I don't know! I didn't deliver it."

The sound of the rain and the scents of soaked wood grew stronger.

Red Raven added, "And I won't even swear that's what the man said. He was muttering. That's what I *thought* he said."

"Did you know him?"

"No, but he must be a member of Water Hickory Clan," he answered a little too glibly. "Don't you agree?"

Feather Dancer thumped his war club into his open palm.

Red Raven glanced up at him. "Then the man ran off after the woman, and I never saw either of them again."

"Why did you go over to the body?"

He shrugged. "It looked odd."

"In what way?"

"Well, for one thing, the man had a sash tied around his throat and his eyes were bulging out of his head." Enthusiastically, he added, "The most interesting part was what the murderer had done—"

"What do you mean, 'murderer'? Short Tail had just attacked a village. He must have been killed in the battle."

Red Raven's lips quirked into a semblance of a

smile, showing his rotted front teeth. "That's what I thought at first, but when I looked closer I saw that all of his belongings, his copper jewelry, his stiletto, bow and quiver, even his clothing had been arranged around him."

Wink sat back on the bench and stared at the ugly little man. "You mean like a Healing Circle?"

Red Raven's smile widened, as though pleased that she'd come to the same conclusion he had. "Curious, isn't it? I can't figure out why a murderer would—"

"One last question," Wink interrupted. "What was the message you were carrying to Short Tail?"

Red Raven blanched. He looked up at Feather Dancer, then across at Long Fin. "High Matron, if Sea Grass ever finds out I told you—"

"What was it?"

Feather Dancer edged closer to Red Raven and searched his skull, as though trying to decide where to land his first blow.

Red Raven hesitated before lifting both hands in surrender. "I was supposed to tell him that his next target was Fan Palm Village."

"Another Loon Nation village!" Long Fin burst out. "But the council voted against attacking any more Loon villages!"

Wink's teeth clenched so hard it set her jaw askew. She longed to stride across Blackbird Town, drag the old woman out of her bed, and slit her throat.

She said, "Feather Dancer, escort Red Raven back to his chamber."

"Certainly, Matron."

Feather Dancer used his club to gesture to the door, and Red Raven hurried out with the warrior close behind him.

Long Fin rubbed his temples as though in pain. "Dear gods, I can't believe it. Sea Grass has defied the council again!"

An odd light-headedness had seized her souls. For a time, she sat there as though made of wood.

"It seems, my son, that Water Hickory Clan is waging its own secret war against the Loon Nation."

She had been trying very hard to prevent civil war, but after this . . .

Long Fin said, "What about the woman that Red Raven saw? Do you think she was Chieftess Sora?"

"Maybe. I'm not sure about that part yet, but I'm almost certain the man was Flint. He recognized Short Tail and said 'our clan.' "

"But if Flint is alive, if he survived the attack on Eagle Flute Village, why hasn't he returned to the Black Falcon Nation?"

Wink shook her head slowly. Dire thoughts had started to weasel into her souls, treachery on a scale she had not imagined.

"There's only one thing that would keep him away."

"What's that?"

A hollow sensation filled her as she answered, "The orders of his clan matron."

5

"Did she—"

"Yes, of course she did!"

The shout woke Sora.

She lay still, listening. How long had she been asleep? It felt like mere moments. Rain pounded through the branches and down upon the ramada like tiny fists. The fragrance of wet pines drenched the air.

"Who was it?" Strongheart asked. "Did you recognize him?"

Sourly, Flint responded, "Not right away."

"Why didn't you tell me about the body? I would have liked to have examined it myself."

Flint just glared at him.

Sora studied the two men who sat ten paces away, beneath a roof of moss-covered oak branches. They made a striking contrast. Flint was tall and muscular, with a handsome chiseled face and long black braid. He wore a plain leather deerhide cape that accented his broad shoulders. Strongheart, though a head taller, looked smaller and thinner. His gaze always seemed to look past a person, as though he lived in a Spirit world no one else could see.

Strongheart repeated, "Who was it? You said you didn't recognize him right away, so eventually you did."

In an icy voice, Flint replied, "Chief Short Tail."

"He was Water Hickory Clan?"

"Yes. She said he'd led the attack."

The lines around Strongheart's eyes deepened. He pulled up the hood of his painted cape and squinted at the sky, watching the rain fall.

Flint rested his balled fists on his knees. "I thought this was over."

"We have just begun, Flint. The Midnight Fox is not dead, just shattered. It's trying as hard as she is to pull itself together."

As though he'd heard, something deep inside Sora stirred. *He is a darkness that listens, that watches.*

Over the winters she had learned that he was not merely darkness. He was a darkness that spoke in the voices of knives.

She rolled to her side and frowned. Lying beside her was a beautiful buffalo-wool cape. She blinked at it, studying the magnificent red and white designs that decorated the collar. It did not belong to her.

Where did I get it? Eagle Flute Village?

From what seemed a great distance a voice whispered, *"I know you killed her, Sora. I know. I know."*

She shook her head, not certain whether she'd heard someone say those words, or she'd only dreamed them.

Flint stabbed a finger at Strongheart. "You're supposed to be the greatest Healer in our world. If you can't bring her reflection-soul back and fix it in her body, tell me, so that I may carry out my duty to protect my people."

His duty. Her belly cramped.

Strongheart drew up one knee and laced his fingers atop it. "Do you think it's time to kill Chieftess Sora?"

"I—I don't know." Flint got to his feet and walked a short distance away. "Maybe."

Emotion tightened her throat. She struggled to stay silent.

"You were married to the chieftess for fourteen winters, Flint. Though you divorced her three winters ago, you told me you still loved her."

"I divorced her because I was afraid I was going to be her next victim! She had murdered so many people, I—"

"No," Strongheart said in a deep voice, "she didn't."

Flint squinted. "Have you lost your senses? She committed her first murder at the age of seven. Her father—"

"Her father killed himself. He was distraught and lonely. He must have thought it was his only way out."

"What are you talking about? She told me herself that she'd killed him."

"Yes, I'm sure she did. All of Chieftess Sora's life her mother led her to believe she'd killed her father by accidentally adding a poisonous plant to the stew she'd made for him. But she did not kill him."

"What about her sister, Walks-among-the-Stars? Sora bashed her brains out with an oar!"

"For three winters, Walks-among-the-Stars lived with the pain of believing Sora had killed their father. She must have heard her mother say it a thousand times. When she could stand it no longer, she took her younger sister, Sora, out in a canoe during a storm to accuse her of murdering their father. Sora had seen ten winters. Perhaps Walks-among-the-Stars meant no harm. All I know is that the two of them began fighting with their oars. Sora struck her older sister in the head, and Walks-among-the-Stars fell out of the canoe and drowned. Sora made it back to shore alive." Strongheart gazed steadily at Flint. "Her sister's death was accidental."

Surprise and disbelief vied on Flint's handsome face. "I'm sure she told you that, but she's lying!"

"I don't think so."

Flint threw up his hands as though exasperated. "What about the murders in Eagle Flute Village, just before the attack? She killed Grown Bear, Black Turtle, and Snail. You're the one who found their bodies!"

Sora's blood went cold. She remembered none of it. But she never did. For twenty-five winters others had had to tell her the things she'd done when in the grips of the Midnight Fox.

Strongheart stared at Flint for such a long time that his dark eyes caught the light and held it like polished mica mirrors. "She was being held captive by those men. She killed them to escape. She was defending herself."

Flint's handsome face slackened. "Blessed gods, you've actually convinced yourself that she's telling the truth. Well, you can deny all the other murders, Priest, but there's one murder you cannot deny. White Fawn's. She killed the woman I was engaged to marry."

Strongheart stared out into the trees, and his brows drew together. "She may have. I'm not sure yet. I—"

"Sora said she did it!"

"Sora said she *thought* she'd done it. She said she remembered 'things,' images."

Flint's fists tightened. "Has your love for her totally blinded you?"

She glanced at Strongheart for confirmation, but the words didn't even seem to affect him. He leaned toward Flint and said, "If she is a murderer, she became one much later in life. The question is, why? What started it?"

Flint propped his hands on his hips. The front of his cape pulled apart, revealing the pale yellow shirt he wore. "You asked me if I still loved her. I do. I always have. That's why I brought her to you. I tried for more than half my life to Heal her. I couldn't."

Less than three moons after Flint had divorced her, Sora's mother, Chieftess Yellow Cypress, had arranged for Sora to marry an elderly Trader named Rockfish. She'd never expected to see Flint again. Then he'd come back and turned her world upside down. He'd given her a powerful sleeping potion and carried her into the Loon Nation, to Eagle Flute Village, in the hopes that Strongheart could Heal her. But she'd been there just a few days when Eagle Flute Village was attacked by warriors from the Water Hickory Clan.

Strongheart said, "Tell me what you did to try and Heal her?"

Flint waved a hand. "Why do you care? I couldn't do it. And, apparently, neither can you. Your efforts have proved no better than mine, or those of her mother."

"Her mother?"

Flint turned and stared at Strongheart. "Yes. Didn't Sora tell you? Her mother was terrified by her attacks. You've seen what happens when the Midnight Fox overtakes her. Sora falls to the ground with her limbs jerking and her teeth gnashing. Throughout her childhood, Sora's mother forced her to see one Healer after another. By the time I met her, at age fourteen, she'd eaten so many Spirit plants that even the smell of them sickened her."

"Has the chieftess ever remembered one of the attacks?"

"She always recalls disconnected images, pieces of things that happened during the killing spree."

Strongheart turned and looked straight into Sora's eyes. Their gazes held. All the kindness in the world seemed to be concentrated in those dark depths.

"One thing you can be certain of," Flint said, "my kinsmen from the Water Hickory Clan are out there hunting for Short Tail's murderer. We can't stay here. We have to leave."

"How would they know he'd been murdered? He must have disappeared during the attack. Surely his clan believes he was killed by Loon warriors."

Flint's jaw hardened. "His warriors would have searched for him—or his body. And they would have found it, just as I did."

"But you had trouble recognizing him. Perhaps they will—"

"They won't have any trouble. Sora did things, bizarre things that will leave no doubt but that he was murdered."

The silence stretched, and the sound of the rain falling through the trees seemed to fill the world.

Finally, Strongheart asked, "What things?"

Flint waved a hand. "She . . . took his possessions . . . and arranged them around him in a circle. My kinsmen will recognize every weapon and piece of jewelry."

"If you knew they'd be recognized, why didn't you take them?"

Flint glared at Strongheart. "I didn't think of it at the time."

Strongheart made a soft thoughtful sound and asked, "Had you ever seen her do something like that before?"

"Yes. Once."

When Flint didn't continue Strongheart took a few moments to study his tormented expression before asking, "When?"

"There was a . . . a pearl Trader." Flint walked a

short distance away, to the edge of the swamp, and gazed out at the rain-stippled water. "I didn't know they were in the council chamber. I walked in on them."

Stunned by his implications, Sora couldn't even speak to defend herself. She stared at him with her mouth open.

Strongheart said, "What were they doing?"

"She was in his arms," he said as though it was still painful to speak of it. "I was furious. I left Blackbird Town and didn't return for two moons. Later, I heard that a woman had found the Trader's body just north of Blackbird Town. She said that every item had been removed from his pack and arranged around the corpse in a circle."

Is it possible that I killed the man and don't remember any of it? Not even what happened in the council chamber before the murder?

Strongheart's voice was mild. "Is that when you gave her the water hemlock that caused her to miscarry your son on the Red Hill?"

Flint went rigid. He slowly lifted his eyes and pinned Strongheart with a deadly look. "Don't ever ask me about that again, Priest. Do you understand? If you ask me about it, I'll kill you."

Strongheart's gaze never wavered. "Flint, we must talk. Just you and I. I can't Heal the chieftess until you have told me—"

"I'm not telling you anything. I'm not the one who's sick. She is."

Strongheart inhaled a deep breath and exhaled the words, "All right. There's only one thing I ask of you: please help me to find a safe place where I can work."

"There's a war going on out there, Priest. There is no safe place."

"The war is between the Black Falcon Nation and the Loon Nation . . . your people and mine. The Sandhill Crane People have not yet taken sides. Nor have the Lily People."

Flint grimaced as though Strongheart were a fool. "But they will, Priest. Soon. And they will side with the Black Falcon Nation. The Lily People will be first; they are the most vulnerable. And the Sandhill Crane territory won't be safe for more than a few days. Here, we are two days from my village, Oak Leaf Village. If we need help, I can go find it. We need to stay where we are."

"I'm taking the chieftess away, Flint. You can accompany us, or not."

Strongheart rose to his feet and walked across the clearing. As he knelt at Sora's side, he gently drew the hide up around her throat. "I think I know a place. Do you feel strong enough to travel? We should leave soon."

She gazed up into his dark eyes. "Yes."

Flint glowered at Strongheart's back and demanded, "Where is this place?"

"There's an ancient village, Forbidden Village, on the shore of Sassafras Lake, north of Minnow Village. It used to be a gathering place for Healers from every nation, but almost no one goes there now." Strongheart helped Sora to her feet. She felt weak, her knees shaky. "It's a Power place, but I believe we'll be safe there."

Flint called, "What makes you think we'll be safe? If it's an old gathering place, everyone knows about it."

Strongheart nodded. "Yes, but only Healers and desperately ill people are brave enough to set foot upon that sacred ground."

"Why?"

He turned to Flint. "It's dangerous to those who do not know its Spirits. After my parents were killed, I spent part of my youth there, studying with an old Healer named Juggler."

Uneasy, Flint said, "Is the old man still there?"

Strongheart shrugged and bent to gather Sora's few belongings, placing them, one by one, into her heavy belt pouch. "I don't even know if he's still alive."

At dusk, they camped near a small cypress pond surrounded by gigantic hackberry trees—one day's walk from Oak Leaf Village. The three of them sat around the fire, silently eating bowls of fish soup.

Strongheart kept a close eye on Flint. He didn't know what Flint expected, but the warrior kept gazing westward, toward Oak Leaf village, as though he desperately needed to run home.

Was he homesick? Or was it something more urgent?

Sora set her bowl down and walked away toward the shore of the pond.

Strongheart gave her some time to be alone, finishing his soup before he followed her.

He found her leaning against the trunk of a hackberry tree, her eyes focused on the sparkflies that blinked amid the branches. Croaking frogs serenaded the night.

"Are you all right?" he asked.

Over her shoulder, she said, "You should be a warrior instead of a priest. You have the skills for it. I didn't hear you approach."

"I think you were occupied with other thoughts."

The tall grass whispered against his leggings as he walked to stand beside her and watch the ducks that silently paddled across the pond in the distance. Silver chevrons bobbed out behind them.

Softly, he reminded, "I asked if you were all right."

She took a deep shaky breath. "I feel broken."

"You will feel that way for a time, until we've found all the pieces."

"Pieces? What pieces?"

"The pieces of your shattered reflection-soul. We've just begun, Sora. For a time, you'll feel like you're looking at yourself in a pool of water."

"Do you truly believe the image will ever be whole again?"

"As we find more and more of the pieces, the picture will begin to coalesce. I think, someday, you will be whole."

Her eyes went hollow, her gaze looking inward at something terrifying. Tears beaded her lashes.

"What is it?" he asked. "Do you need me?"

She closed her eyes, and he sensed that she longed to tell him how very much she needed him, but she would not. Could not. She was the high chieftess of the Black Falcon Nation. He was an enemy priest.

She said, "Will you stay with me? Help me to find the pieces?"

"Sora, please look at me."

She opened her eyes and swallowed hard before she turned to face him. The reflected light of the pond shimmered over her beautiful face.

"I'll stay," he said softly, "but I want you to know that I'm afraid."

"Of me?" Her voice shook. "I don't blame you, I—"

"No, Sora. I'm not afraid of you. I've never feared you."

Their gazes held, and she looked at him with more longing than any woman ever had.

He lifted a hand to comfortingly brush the hair away from her face. "The time is coming, very soon, when the Midnight Fox will seek me out. I pray that my heart is not too small to understand what he tells me."

A single tear ran down her right cheek. She did not blink, just stared at him.

Finally, she said, "I pray you survive."

"I will."

She stepped forward and before he realized what was happening, she hugged him hard enough to drive the breath from his lungs. "Don't be so certain," she whispered. "There's only one person who's looked into the Fox's eyes and lived."

"I know, but Flint didn't realize what he was dealing

with. I do." He wrapped his arms around her, and she seemed to melt against him.

The experience of looking into his wife's eyes and seeing a malignant Spirit staring back had almost torn Flint apart. The next day, he'd divorced her and run home to Oak Leaf Village.

Sora gently pushed away from Strongheart, gave him a heartrending look, and walked back to their camp, where Flint still sat finishing his soup. Flint said something to her and she responded, but their voices were too faint for Strongheart to make out the words.

He turned and watched the sparkflies glitter over the pond.

7

"War Chief?" the guard outside his door called.

Feather Dancer sat up in his blankets and blinked the sleep from his eyes. "What is it, Clearwing?"

"Someone is coming."

Feather Dancer threw back his blankets and reached for his brown shirt. As he slipped it over his head, he looked around. His house was small in comparison to the other elite buildings in Blackbird Town, fifteen paces square, but the roof soared four times the height of a man, giving it the appearance of being much larger. The coals in the fire hearth still gleamed, casting a reddish glow over the log walls.

It had to be two or three hands of time before dawn.

He strapped his war belt around his waist and

adjusted the weapons tied to it: a deer-bone stiletto, war club, and red chert knife.

"War Chief, it's the high matron. She's walking fast, and she's *alone*."

Feather Dancer grabbed his sandals and quickly laced them up. When he ducked beneath the door curtain, he saw her. She wore a black cape with the hood up, but moonlight shone from her round face and narrow nose. Even if it hadn't, he would recognize her walk anywhere.

"Hurry," he told Clearwing. "Get down there and escort her."

Clearwing rushed down the stairs that adorned the front of the War Chief's Mound and ran out into the plaza to meet the high matron.

Feather Dancer's gaze scanned the town. Even in the dim light, he could see the seven pyramid-shaped mounds that framed the plaza. Massive log buildings with peaked roofs adorned the mound tops. His gaze drifted down to the lake, where hundreds of tiny thatched houses lined the shore. An assassin would most likely secret himself among the commoners where it would be harder to spot him.

The high matron came up the steps with Clearwing right behind her, and Feather Dancer bowed and said, "Matron, I thought we decided you wouldn't go anywhere alone for a while. Where are your guards?"

Feather Dancer had posted two of his best men outside her bedchamber.

"I ordered them not to accompany me." She gestured to his door. "May I?"

"Of course, Matron," he said, and held the curtain aside for her to enter.

After she'd ducked into his house, Feather Dancer gestured to Clearwing, signaling him to keep standing guard outside the door. Clearwing resumed his former position. He was medium-sized man with a square face and serious eyes—a good man, and an excellent warrior.

For a few days, while Feather Dancer was being held captive in Eagle Flute Village, Clearwing had been elevated to the position of war chief of the Black Falcon Nation—a position he had lost when Feather Dancer escaped the village massacre and returned to Blackbird Town. Lesser men would have felt resentful, or worse, at the demotion. But Clearwing seemed unaffected.

Feather Dancer stepped through his door and let the curtain fall closed behind him.

The matron stood in front of the hearth with her hands extended to the faint warmth of the glowing coals.

Feather Dancer walked over, knelt by the woodpile, and pulled out a branch. As he scraped the coals into a pile in the middle of the hearth, he said, "What happened?"

Matron Wink shoved her hood back, and he could see she still wore her yellow sleepshirt. A frizzy graying black braid fell over her right shoulder. She must have risen straight from her blankets.

"I've been thinking about our conversation with Red Raven," she said. The lines around her ample mouth cut deeper.

"What about it?" He placed branches on top of the coals and blew on them until flames crackled to life around the new tinder.

As though she couldn't stand still, she paced in front of the fire. "Let's assume that the man and woman he saw in Eagle Flute Village were Flint and Sora. Didn't it strike you as unlikely that they would have willingly returned to the village after the attack?"

"It struck me as impossible," he said, and tossed another branch onto the flames. A fluttering yellow gleam filled his house, casting their shadows over the walls like leaping giants.

Matron Wink stopped pacing to stare at him. "Why did you think it was impossible?"

"Flint was once a warrior, a good one. He would have never gone back, Matron. It was too dangerous."

Wink countered, "Perhaps he went back searching for Sora."

"Yes, that's possible. But I doubt it."

Her dark eyes searched his face. "Why didn't you tell me these suspicions?"

He rose to his feet and rested his hand on the hilt of his belted stiletto. "I'm not sure they matter."

"What do you mean? Of course they matter. What if—"

"They only matter, Matron, if they are true."

She frowned for several moments before she said, "You're right. Do you think Red Raven was lying?"

"My gut tells me he wasn't. But my gut isn't always the best judge of these things. I wish we had more information."

"Well, we don't." She massaged her temples as though a headache pounded behind her eyes. "What does your gut tell you about Flint?"

Feather Dancer hesitated, not certain he wanted to say. At volatile times such as these, opinions could be as dangerous as weapons. He clenched his fists to keep his emotions bottled up. "Matron, he betrayed Chieftess Sora to the Loon People. After his cohorts ambushed us on the trail, and we were taken as hostages to Eagle Flute Village, I watched him closely. He is a coward and a liar. I don't trust him."

"Which means . . . what?"

He shifted, uneasy. "I've been asking myself if perhaps Flint wasn't surprised to see Chieftess Sora at Eagle Flute Village. The way Red Raven told the story it sounded as though he might have been."

"Are you suggesting that—that he didn't go there looking for her? That he went there for another reason?"

"It's one of many possibilities I've been considering."

"What other reason could he have had?"

Feather Dancer lifted a shoulder and stared at the flames dancing around the logs. The wet wood smoked badly. As though alive, blue-gray clouds rose from the fire hearth and crawled across the roof, waiting to be sucked out through the smokehole.

Softly, she replied, "Blessed gods, if he went there deliberately, it must have been to meet someone, and that means . . ." Her eyes narrowed.

Feather Dancer finished the sentence: "The meeting had been arranged either before the attack, or in the confusion just after."

She sank down onto the log bench in front of the fire. "Blessed Ancestors, I'm beginning to fear that she's smarter than I am. She's outmaneuvered me at every turn."

Feather Dancer gave her a few moments before he said, "Matron, this is a very dangerous time. Please promise me that you will not leave your house again without a guard."

She lowered her face into her hands and nodded.

8

RED RAVEN GLANCED AT THE TWO GUARDS POSTED on either side of the door, then looked around the large chamber. Thirty paces square and constructed of upright logs more than four times the height of a man, it was a beautiful place, a place that befitted the status of the matron of the Water Hickory Clan. Torches cast a flickering yellow gleam over the painted rawhide shields that hung along the walls, each representing a sacred event in the history of the clan.

He wandered around looking into the crushed shell and jet eyes of the long-lost heroes depicted on the shields. There was Skyholder, the Creator, holding a water hickory sapling in his left hand and a rock in his right hand. The rock cast a long shadow across the painting, pointing westward. After he'd created the world, Skyholder had flown down from the stars to inspect it. There was no nighttime, because he hadn't created it yet, so it was always dawn. He started in the far east, creating rivers, oceans, mountains, and planting trees as he went. His favorite tree was the water hickory—or that's the version of the story his clan told. However, if he'd happened to be in the Bald Cypress Clan's Matron's House she would have said it was the bald cypress tree. The two things no one argued about were that Skyholder's favorite animal was the duck known as the shoveler, who helped him create the world, and that he was led across the land by the shadow of the rock, which always pointed due west. That's how the four main clans of the Black Falcon Nation came to be named: Water Hickory Clan, Bald Cypress Clan, Shoveler Clan, and the Shadow Rock Clan. For as far back as anyone could remember the clans had bickered over which was Skyholder's favorite clan. Personally, he thought . . .

Red Raven jumped when the door curtain to the council chamber was drawn back.

Sea Grass—matron of Water Hickory Clan—hobbled across the council chamber toward him, followed by her ever-present personal guards. The old woman had her white hair twisted into a bun on top of her head. Her thin face and beaked nose looked sallow, as though all the color had been leached out, but her clothing was extraordinary. She wore a deep blue dress decorated with several hundred small circlets of polished conch shell that flashed in the torchlight. Both guards wore plain brown knee-length shirts, but a variety of weapons adorned their belts: stilettos, knives, war clubs.

"Matron," he said, and bowed to her. "It is good to see you looking so well."

"Stop patronizing me and sit down," she ordered.

"Of—of course, Matron." He sat on one of the four log benches that framed the central fire hearth.

Sea Grass grunted as she eased down to the bench opposite him and held her hands out to the fire. Her fingers looked more like translucent claws than parts of a human body. Her guards took up positions a short distance away.

"High Matron Wink has been on a tirade," she said, wasting no time. "I've had to do some fancy talking to convince the Council of Elders not to outcast Water Hickory Clan from the nation. Thank the gods that Matron Wigeon is a scared rabbit, or no one would have been on my side. As it was, we were lucky. Chief Long Fin abstained from the vote, leaving the council divided: Wigeon and I against, Black Birch and Wink for."

Red Raven made the appropriate *tsk tsk* sound. "It sounds terrible, Matron. I can see you're in a difficult position, but what does that have to do with me?"

Her old eyes blazed. "Matron Wink knows more than she's saying. I want to know where she heard it from."

Red Raven straightened in surprise. "What do you mean?"

"I mean"—Sea Grass gave him the evil eye—"that

two nights ago, one of my spies saw Feather Dancer drag you out of your blankets and escort you to Matron Wink's house. What did you tell her?"

Red Raven wet his dry lips. His nose had begun to twitch, as it always did when he was nervous. "Nothing, Matron. She questioned me, of course, but I swear I told her nothing. At least, nothing important."

She pointed a crooked finger at him. "If you lie to me once more, I'll have your heart cut out and left bleeding on the floor. What did she ask you?"

He glanced at the guards. He had to tell Sea Grass enough information to satisfy her, but not so much that she'd carry out her threat. "She told me that she'd heard I was the one who found Chief Short Tail. I don't know how she knew it, but she did, and she—"

"You're such a braggart, by the time you left my chamber, everyone for three days' walk knew it. What else did she say? And for the sake of the gods, stop twitching your nose! It's infernally annoying."

He swallowed hard. "She wanted to know about the woman I'd seen in the forest before I discovered the body."

"And?"

"I told her almost nothing! She wanted to know what the woman looked like, and I said it was dark, I couldn't really tell, except that she was tall and had long black hair."

Sea Grass' wrinkles rearranged into worried lines.

"Did you tell her why you'd gone to Eagle Flute Village?"

"Of course not! What do think I am, a traitor?"

She stared at him as though trying to decide if she should just kill him now and get it over with, or question him further. "Did Wink ask any questions about Short Tail?"

"No."

"None? She didn't even slyly mention the fact that he'd openly opposed me over the Eagle Flute Village attack?"

Red Raven cocked his head. "I don't think she knows about it, Matron. *I* didn't even know about it."

Sea Grass folded her clawlike hands in her lap and seemed to be thinking about that. "All she did was ask about the woman?"

"Yes, Matron. She asked me if I'd recognized her. I told her no, it was too dark. Next she asked me about the woman's voice. Had I ever heard it before. I told her it did sound familiar, but that I hadn't actually recognized it."

Sea Grass rubbed her jaw. "I wonder . . ."

"Wonder what, Matron?"

She gave him a look that would have silenced the gods. "Never interrupt me."

Red Raven clamped his jaw.

"Wink has been desperate to find Chieftess Sora. She's sent out so many search parties I've lost count. They've found nothing, of course."

The way she said "of course" made Red Raven think she had known they wouldn't. Perhaps because the high chieftess was dead. That's what everyone thought. Speculation ran rampant that she'd been burned alive in one of the lodges at Eagle Flute Village, or shot down during the battle and eaten by wolves—as was her just due. After all, the chieftess had murdered Matron Sea Grass' son, War Chief Skinner.

It was an embarrassing event. Matron Wink's nephew, Far Eye, had found War Chief Skinner lying dead in the forest beside the chieftess. Clearly Skinner had tried to kill her; his fingers were still wrapped around her throat. Apparently, the chieftess had managed to slip poison into Skinner's cup and when he'd started to feel it, he'd attacked her.

Sea Grass had been hysterical over the death of her only son. She'd wanted revenge. It was customary for the victim's family to claim the life of the murderer, or a member of the murderer's family; it was the Law of Retribution. But everyone knew that Sea Grass would never get her hands on the high chieftess of the Black Falcon Nation, and out of respect, Water Hickory Clan could not claim another member of the Shadow Rock Clan—mostly because they were the ruling clan.

As a result, Sea Grass had never been fairly compensated for the loss of her son—a fact that Sea Grass mentioned whenever she was negotiating with High Matron Wink, trying to get her to make concessions that benefited Water Hickory Clan.

Sea Grass clenched her jaw for several moments before she said, "What else did Wink ask you?"

"Nothing, Matron. That was all. She wanted to know about the woman, and after I told her everything I knew, she let me go."

Sea Grass' eyes narrowed. She aimed that crooked finger at him again. "You'd better be telling me the truth."

"I am! I give you my oath!"

"As if that would convince me," Sea Grass said caustically.

"Well, Matron, what else can I say?"

The smile that came to her wrinkled lips made him wish he hadn't asked that question.

Sea Grass waved to her guards. "Leave us alone. I wish to speak with Red Raven in private."

The guards left.

Sea Grass glowered at him for so long that Red Raven's heart almost climbed out of his throat. When she wanted to, she could look like one of the evil Earth Spirits who roamed the forests in search of fresh human meat.

"I knew the story you told me when you returned from Eagle Flute Village was a half-truth, but it didn't matter . . . until now."

In the most innocent voice he could muster, Red Raven said, "Matron, truly, I don't know what you mean. I am your most loyal—"

"Stop it, or I'll call my guards back in and have them puncture your lungs."

He went silent.

She continued, "Rumor has it that High Matron Wink has organized a secret meeting with the other clan matrons, a meeting to which I am not invited. What did you tell her that led her to such desperate action?"

Red Raven squirmed. He couldn't help it. He felt like a bug skewered with a cactus thorn for a child's amusement. "The high matron can be . . . very persuasive. . . ."

Her thin white eyebrows pulled down over her beaked nose. "*What* did you tell her?"

He had to think fast or he would not walk out of this chamber alive. "Something that I—I did not tell you, Matron. I was too afraid to tell you."

"Yes?"

He glanced around the chamber before hissing, "I saw a man, Matron. I didn't know him. He came out of the trees, breathing hard, saw the woman, and said, 'What are you doing here? I told you I'd take care of it!'"

"What did the woman say? And I want every word," she said precisely.

The story poured out of his mouth: "She said, 'He defied our matron. He deserved more than just death.'"

A small satisfied smile came to Sea Grass' wrinkled lips. "And?"

Red Raven hesitated. Even though this was a version of the truth, it still might get him killed. "The man said,

'Now there won't be anyone to tell our clan matron I received her message.' "

Sea Grass' eyes narrowed. "Why didn't you tell me that part?"

"Matron"—he wiped his sweating brow on his sleeve—"I wasn't sure it was him, and I didn't want to call out and have an enemy arrow stick in my back. That's why I told you I hadn't seen him and . . . and why I couldn't deliver your message."

Her old voice went low and ominous. "But you could have."

"*If* I'd been sure it was him! I wasn't!"

She seemed to be mulling that over. "What did Wink say when you told her this part of the story?"

"She asked me what the message was, and I said I hadn't delivered it. Which you know is true, Matron." The acrid smell of his own sweat was becoming overpowering. He added, "Then she asked me if I knew the man. I said, *truthfully,* that I did not."

Sea Grass' gaze drifted over the chamber, as though contemplating every possible permutation of the high matron's thoughts. In a voice so soft that Red Raven suspected she didn't realize he could hear her, she said, "But Wink knew who the man was. Of course she did. Who else could he have been? This very instant she must be trying to fathom what I'm up to. Which means . . ."

Her gaze came back to Red Raven. His shoulders knotted, as though they could already hear bow strings being pulled tight. "You may still be useful."

Relief flooded his veins with such intensity he sagged forward on the bench. "Command me and I'll be on my way, Matron. I'll do whatever you wish me to."

"Yes," she said with a cold smile. "I know you will."

9

As Mother Sun descended toward the western horizon, an iridescent copper gleam suffused the
forest, shimmering from the magnolia leaves and
falling across the trail like shattered bits of amber.

Sora shoved another low-hanging branch aside and
continued up the trail behind Flint and Strongheart. No
one had come this way in a long time. For most of the
day, they'd been hacking and ripping at the overgrown
shrubs and vines that blocked the trail. Often, they'd
just given up and found a way around.

She gazed up at the green canopy. It had been a
silent trip, each of them focused on getting out of the
Black Falcon Nation, but as dusk settled upon the land,
Sora could tell that solace was about to end. Ahead of
her, Flint and Strongheart walked side by side. Flint

kept sneaking glances at Strongheart, who pretended not to notice.

Finally, Flint said, "Is the story about the Meteorite People true?"

"Which story?"

Flint turned to scowl at the tall slender holy man. "What do you mean 'which story?' The story about you calling down the Meteorite People to crush a village elder you didn't like. I heard they found a grand total of six pieces of the poor man."

She couldn't see Strongheart's face, but she heard him sigh. "I did dislike him, but I did not call down the Meteorite People who struck him."

"Then who did?"

"I don't know. The gods, perhaps."

"Hmm," Flint said in a disbelieving voice. "What about the soul-flying stories? It is said that you can send your soul flying to attack your enemies."

"Who says?"

"Does it matter?"

"It matters to me."

As though he hadn't heard, Flint said, "A Trader told me there was a very disagreeable clan matron in the south who saw you soul-flying. Her family found her the next morning with her guts hanging out of her mouth. Apparently she'd vomited them up."

"Did it occur to you that she may have been so disagreeable a member of her own village stuffed the entrails down her throat and blamed me to escape the wrath of her relatives?"

"Are you saying that all of the stories about your Spirit Powers are false?"

Strongheart stopped in the middle of the trail and stared at him. "You're not afraid of me, are you, Flint?"

Flint spread his legs as though to brace himself against a Spirit attack. "Of course not. I wouldn't have brought Sora to you if I'd been afraid of you."

"Nor would you if you'd thought the stories were false."

They walked in silence again for a few paces before Strongheart said, "Now, may I ask you some questions?"

Flint gave him an askance look and stopped again. "What about?"

Strongheart stopped beside him. "Did you know Chief Short Tail would return to Eagle Flute Village?"

Flint's jaw dropped open. "Of course not. How could I have known?"

"I thought perhaps you were waiting for him."

"Is your soul out wandering? That's insane!" Flint replied in irritation.

"I can't fathom any other reason you would have returned to the burned village—except to meet someone."

"Are you accusing me of conspiring—"

"With your own relatives?" Strongheart interrupted. "Yes, I am. Were you?"

Sora strode forward, shouldered between the men, and said, "I'm tired. I would like to reach Sassafras Lake before it's completely dark—which is not going to happen if you two keep stopping in the middle of the trail."

As she marched ahead of them, they fell into line behind her. Flint grumbled what sounded like a taunt beneath his breath. Strongheart did not respond.

As they walked through the cool shadows of the magnolias, Strongheart said, "Forbidden Village is just up ahead. Why don't you let me lead the way, Chieftess?"

Sora slowed her pace. As he passed by her, he lightly brushed her arm with his hand; it was a comforting pat, nothing more, but . . .

Flint grabbed her arm and pulled her backward so hard she almost lost her footing. He allowed Strongheart to get twenty paces ahead before he whispered, "When he goes to sleep tonight, we should slip away."

"I don't want to slip away."

"He's been trying to Heal you for a quarter moon. I was wrong to bring you to him. He isn't Powerful enough to Heal you. Let me take you north to Priest Long Lance. I studied with him. I know he'll remember me and agree to Heal you."

"Many people consider Long Lance to be a witch."

"He's a very great Healer. He taught me everything he knew about Spirit Plants and Healing techniques," he said, but she sensed there was more to it, some deep undercurrent of emotion that she couldn't define. His grip tightened, as though if she refused to go away with him he would drag her against her will.

"No, Flint."

Strongheart had followed the trail around a dense

briar and disappeared. A thread of fear wound through her, as it always did when he was out of her sight.

She pulled her arm away from Flint and tried to catch up with Strongheart.

"I love you," Flint called. "Why won't you come with me?"

"I can't, I—"

He ran, grabbed her shoulder hard, and whirled her around to look at him. "Is it because you love him?" His voice was hateful.

"Flint, for the sake of the gods, stop this! Can't you see that every time Strongheart touches me the Midnight Fox cowers? It knows he can kill it. I must give him more time."

"Are you saying you don't love him?"

"I'm saying I believe he can Heal me." She shoved his hand away and continued walking.

Beyond the briar, the trail cut across a grassy meadow and opened onto the shore of Sassafras Lake, where bald cypresses flourished in the deep green water.

She didn't see Strongheart and started to . . .

The hair on the back of her neck suddenly prickled, and her eyes instinctively drifted to the right. Amid a weave of massive moss-covered trunks, she glimpsed Strongheart's face. He seemed to be staring at something in the distance.

"What's he looking at?" Flint asked.

"I can't tell."

As she walked forward, Forbidden Village came into view. It must have been beautiful at one time, long ago, before the forest had overgrown the thatched lodges. Now, the vine-covered ruins scattered the lakeshore for as far as she could see.

"Strongheart?" she called.

He turned, and the shadows cast by the trees crisscrossed his round face like charcoal filigree. His hooked nose seemed longer, his bulging eyes huge. He tucked a lock of black hair behind his ear and pointed to an overgrown lodge ten paces away. Saplings had sprouted in front of the doorway. "That used to be my home, when I studied with Juggler."

Flint stepped forward, glanced at it, and said, "Well, nobody's been here for a long time. The old man must be dead."

Pain flickered in Strongheart's eyes. "Yes, or moved on." He went to kneel in front of the lodge's doorway, where he pushed away the saplings and peered inside. After several heartbeats he said, "All of his belongings are still here. Every pot rests in the same place I remember. I wonder what happened."

Sora winced at the hurt in his voice. He might just as easily have said, *I wonder if he was sick and needed me, and I wasn't here.*

Flint kicked at a moss-covered pole that had once been part of the lodge frame. "Who cares? He's gone, and this is no place for us. Let's leave before it's too dark to travel. I still think we ought to stay close to Oak Leaf Village."

Evening light penetrated the branches and illumined

the clouds of membranous wings that moved through the trees, glowing with a faint lavender hue.

Sora knelt beside Strongheart. Inside the lodge, she saw a row of pots sealed with boiled pine pitch on the rear wall. A frown lined her forehead.

"That's strange," she said. "Why haven't the vines filled this lodge and covered the pots?"

In a reverent voice, Strongheart answered, "Juggler's Power is still here, keeping them at bay. Every night he used to breathe part of his souls into these walls. Do you feel him?"

Sora *did* feel something; it was like downy cotton being rubbed against the skin, warm and soft. "I think so."

"He was a good man," Strongheart said as he rose to his feet. "I pray that he died quietly, without pain."

She looked up at him and saw the glimmer of tears in his eyes before he turned away. It surprised her, until she realized that Juggler must have been like a father to him after the deaths of his parents. He'd probably been looking forward to seeing his old teacher.

To Flint, Strongheart said, "We're staying here. Tonight we'll camp on the lakeshore; then tomorrow we'll begin rebuilding Juggler's lodge."

"What!" Flint objected. "I'm not staying here. This place is an overgrown ruin."

Strongheart went to a nearby dead tree and began cracking off the lowest branches, gathering dry wood to make their supper fire.

Sora rose to help him, but Flint said, "Don't tell me

you're going to put up with this? You're the high chieftess of the Black Falcon Nation! You should be lying on a bed of soft buffalohides with a dozen slaves tending your needs, not here in this . . . this . . . moldering old village. You need better care. You need a great Healer."

She held his gaze. "I have a great Healer. Leave if you want to. No one is holding you here."

"Blessed gods!" he hissed. "Don't you see what he's doing? He's trying to turn you against me!"

His jealousy was progressively getting worse, turning to hatred.

Sora walked to another tree and began cracking off dead branches, cradling them in the crook of her left arm.

Flint thrashed away through the brush. When she turned to look, he was gone.

"Don't worry," Strongheart said. "He'll be back. He loves you."

"Does he?" A hollow ache expanded in her chest, as though listening to Flint had eaten out her insides.

"Yes. And you love him."

She hesitated for an instant before replying, "I've loved him for as long as I can remember."

Strongheart gave her a sad smile and went to lay his branches in a clearing near the water. As he arranged the kindling over a nest of dry leaves, he said, "Come and sit by me. Let's talk."

She carried her branches over, placed them on the pile with his, and sat down cross-legged on the sand.

The earthy scents of evening had begun to filter through the forest. Out in the middle of the lake, a fish jumped. Silver rings bobbed away after the splash.

"You must be tired," he said. "We had a long day."

"I am tired, and hungry."

"Me, too."

He removed his firebow from his belt pouch and placed the tip in a punky piece of wood. As the bow spun, the soft wood began to smoke. He dumped the embers onto the dry leaves and blew on them. In less than fifty heartbeats smoke rose from the leaves, and fire crackled to life. He rearranged the kindling, making certain that the flames licked at the wood, then sank down beside her.

"I'm sorry," he said, "about all the arguing."

"You think Flint's presence is a hindrance to my Healing, don't you?"

He didn't answer for a time. He just watched the last remnants of sunlight sparkle on the lake. "You once told me that his presence made you feel safe. Is that still true?"

Beautiful memories of lying with Flint in fragrant spring grass, loving each other all day long, filled her. She could feel his touch as clearly today as she had eighteen winters ago.

"We've loved each other since we were fourteen winters. Though I've lived the past three winters without him, he's never been out of my thoughts. I—"

"That's not what I asked you," he gently reminded.

"No, I—I know that." She uneasily studied her hands. "Do you recall the conversation we had about the 'dangerous things'?"

"Yes. You said that the dangerous things slip from their hidden chambers and walk around your souls while Flint is loving you."

She nodded. "That's the only time I feel safe enough to look at them. In his arms."

Strongheart put a hand against her hair to force her to look at him and tenderly said, "Then it doesn't matter whether I think he's a hindrance or not. You need him here."

He untied his belt pouch and opened the laces, smiling at her as he drew out a soot-coated tea pot, tripod, and two wooden cups. "What kind of tea do you prefer?"

"I don't care. Whatever you want."

A rustling sounded as he searched his pouch and drew out a small leather bag. "While we were walking today, I gathered several herbs. I hope you like this mixture." He pulled open the laces and handed the bag to her.

She held it to her nose. "Umm, it smells wonderful. What is it?"

"A variety of blossoms. But I also added some palm sap crystals to sweeten it."

He picked up the tea pot and went to the lake to dip it full of water. As he walked back, his cape swayed around his long legs.

"Let's talk while I make the tea."

"I'd like that," she said.

"I know Flint is a member of Water Hickory Clan, and that he was born in Oak Leaf Village," Strongheart said. "But I know almost nothing else about him. Does he have brothers or sisters?"

He poured some of the herbs into the water, then placed it at the edge of the flames.

The question caught her off guard. "I thought you wanted to ask questions about me."

"Let's talk about Flint first."

She gestured uncertainly. "Very well, but there isn't much to tell. He had three brothers, but they all died before Flint had seen four winters. I don't think he even remembers them."

"What about his father?"

"He died just after Flint was born. The entire time we were married, I never heard Flint speak of him."

Strongheart's brows pulled together. He laid another branch on the fire and frowned at the flames. "What about his mother?"

"She was a weaver. A good one. She made some beautiful shirts and capes for Flint while we were married."

"For Flint? Not for you?"

"For Flint."

Strongheart just blinked. "Is she still alive?"

"I don't know. After he divorced me, I lost contact with her. She and I never—"

"Chieftess, do you think Flint returned to Eagle Flute Village to meet someone? A member of his clan?"

The sudden change of topics brought a flood of disconnected images: Flint's face very close to hers . . . his scent, a combination of woodsmoke and damp earth . . . the sound of his whispers. . . .

Strongheart pressed, "Why else would he have returned to the village?"

"I don't know. Perhaps to tend to the bodies of his dead relatives."

Strongheart seemed to deflate a little. He sat back on the sand. "I hadn't thought of that. But it is possible. Eventually, I will return to do that for my family."

Somewhere in the distance, Thunderbirds rumbled and their calls echoed through the trees. The scent of rain filled the air.

He reached for a branch and prodded the fire again. Flames leaped around the pot. "Perhaps my grief has clouded my perception of him."

She curled her legs around her hips, and gazed out at Sassafras Lake. Evening had blushed color into the windblown waves, turning them a pale purple. "Strongheart, I want you to tell me the truth about something. Will you do that?"

The lines at the corners of his eyes deepened. He looked as though he was afraid she would ask him a question that he dared not answer at this stage of her Healing, but he said, "Yes. I will. What is it?"

"What's wrong with me? Can't you find my reflection-soul and bring it back to my body?"

"It's more complicated. I think you have a ghost sickness."

"A ghost sickness?"

"Yes. A ghost person is sending you evil dreams that drive away your soul. That's what the Midnight Fox is."

"Evil dreams? Like the dream about the Red Hill?"

"Yes."

She mulled that over. "Who is the ghost?"

"I don't know. I need to talk with you more. There are questions I must ask, and I haven't been able to."

"Because of Flint?"

Strongheart's mouth tightened. "He thinks he's protecting you. He won't let me get very close."

She lifted her head and found him studying her with glistening brown eyes. "He's always been jealous. And it's getting worse."

"Yes. I know."

In warning, she said, "You'll have to be very careful, or he'll—"

"Hurt us."

She nodded.

As the evening deepened, the hoarse cries of night herons filtered through the trees.

"Sora, I have something that might help me to determine if it's a spell or a ghost sickness, but I've been waiting for the right time before suggesting it."

She waited for him to say more, but when he didn't she asked, "What is it?"

He reached for his belt pouch and pulled out a small red bag. "This is a special tea. It . . ." He appeared to be thinking about how to describe it. "It opens a doorway."

"A doorway to what?"

He swiveled around to face her. "I put this bag in my belt pouch just before the attack on Eagle Flute Village. I was bringing it to you when—when I found the warriors who'd been guarding you."

"Black Turtle and Snail. The men I murdered."

"I think that's the wrong word, Chieftess."

"Do you?"

"Yes. You heard what I told Flint this morning. I don't think you murdered Black Turtle or Snail, or many of the people you're accused of murdering, including your father and your sister. Your father killed himself. All of the others, except for perhaps White Fawn, either died accidentally, or you killed to protect yourself." He placed another stick on the flames and leaned forward to blow on it. "You've been able to recall so few details about White Fawn's death I have no way of knowing what really happened."

"What about Short Tail?"

He cocked his head uncertainly. "I don't know yet."

Her eyes blurred. All of her life she'd been told she was a murderer. She'd grown up believing it.

He held up the red bag. "I haven't given this to you yet, because it's dangerous. I believe it may drive away the Midnight Fox, but I'll need to watch you. The proper dose varies from person to person."

"It's a Spirit Plant," she said in a disheartened voice. "I hate Spirit Plants."

"It's a combination of swamp cabbage root and ground thorn apple seeds. Not only is it a pathway for understanding illness, it's the best cure for the Rainbow Black."

Even from here she could smell the bitter odor wafting from the bag. "It must taste bad."

"Fortunately, not as bad as it smells."

She smiled. "Brew it. I . . . I'll drink it."

"Soon." He tucked it back into his pouch. "When Flint returns. I'll need his help."

"Do you think he'll give it? Or just argue about whether or not it's the right thing to do?"

With a disheartened sigh, he said, "Oh, a little of both, I imagine."

FEATHER DANCER DREW BACK THE DOOR CURTAIN on the Matron's House and looked out across the dark plaza of Blackbird Town. "You go first, Matron. I'll be right behind you."

Wink stepped out beneath the eaves and watched the rain sheet out of the night sky. She couldn't see farther than twenty paces, but her gaze instinctively moved to the seven mounds that composed the heart of the town. The only light that penetrated the downpour came from the Chieftess' Mound, in front of her, where the eternal fire burned.

"I hope the others are already there," she said as she flipped up the hood of her black feathered cape.

"They should be. You were wise to instruct each person to arrive at a different time. The Priest's House is the one place in Blackbird Town where people might go at any time of day or night."

As he gazed into the darkness, the white ridges of scars that covered his face rearranged into anxious lines.

"Don't worry," she said. "It's as black as boiled pine pitch out here. If there's an assassin waiting for me, he's not going to see me any sooner than I see him."

Feather Dancer pulled his war club from his belt. "The difference, Matron, is that he, or she, knows you have to walk out of this house sometime."

She gave him a halfhearted smile. "If he succeeds, make sure Sea Grass is next, will you?"

He nodded gravely, and she strode out into the rain, heading for the stairs cut into the face of the Matron's Mound. Wind whipped her cape around her legs.

They descended the stairs and started across the plaza. Ahead, she saw the faint glimmering of Persimmon Lake and the dark outline of the Priest's Mound.

Being out in the open, even in this drenching rain, made her spine tingle. If she hadn't already, after tonight, Matron Sea Grass would almost certainly hire an assassin to eliminate not only Wink, but every other clan matron in the Black Falcon Nation who voted with Wink.

As she hurried by the Chieftess' Mound, Wink's heart ached. She missed Sora desperately. For more than twenty-five winters, Sora had comforted, guided, and advised her. In the worst of times, she had laughed

away Wink's fears and straightened reality for her.
Right now, she needed Sora more than she had ever
needed her in her life.

Gods, Sora, I pray you're safe.

Feather Dancer's steps padded less than one pace
behind her as she climbed the steps of Priest Teal's
mound. When they neared the doorway, a faint orange
gleam penetrated the rain, and the elaborate paintings
that decorated the clay-plastered walls came into view:
life-size images of dancing Birdmen, mountain lions
with the feet of eagles, and coiled snakes with human
smiles.

The Priest's House was separated into two chambers. In the front, there was a small chamber with a
sleeping bench, fire hearth, and other essentials, but
there was a doorway in the rear that opened into the
charnel house, the place where Teal prepared the dead
for the journey to the afterlife. Row upon row of clean
dry bones rested on the wall shelves. Tucked into
ceramic pots, or wrapped in cloth bundles, they rep-
resented the last remains of centuries of elite rulers.
Wink frequently came here, as did every other matron,
to seek advice from her ancestor's eye-souls, the souls
that remained with the bodies forever.

She stopped in front of the door curtain. "Teal?"

A hoarse old voice answered, "Come, Matron."

Ducking beneath the curtain, she found him sitting on
a mat before the hearth, sipping a cup of tea. Three
other people sat around the fire: her son, Chief Long
Fin; Matron Birch from the Bald Cypress Clan; and

Matron Wigeon from the Shoveler Clan. Both old women had gray hair and shriveled faces. Birch clutched her walking stick across her lap. Her son looked frightened, as though he suspected she was about to initiate civil war between the clans and nothing he said would make any difference.

"Thank you all for coming," Wink said as she untied her black cape, shook the rain from it, and hung it on one of the pegs by the door.

"None of us has any choice in the matter, do we?" Matron Birch said. She wore a beautiful tan dress scalloped with freshwater pearls.

"No," Wink answered. "I don't think so."

Priest Teal leaned forward and gestured to the one unoccupied mat on the opposite side of the fire near Long Fin. "Please join us, High Matron." His bald head and age-bowed back reminded her of a plucked bird.

"Thank you, Teal." As she crossed the floor to the mat, Wink smoothed her hands over her plain black dress.

Feather Dancer inspected the room and walked to the rear of the house, where he drew back the door curtain to the charnel chamber to look inside. While he completed his search, Wink studied the life-size images of the gods that danced around the walls. Teal seemed to paint a new one every winter, and now a crowd of divine eyes gazed down upon her.

"May I pour you a cup of tea?" Teal asked.

"Yes, thank you, Teal."

He had a sunken skeletal face and white-filmed eyes that glowed eerily in the firelight. He dipped up a cup and handed it around the fire to her.

She took it and smelled the sweet aroma of prickly pear fruit wafting up with the steam.

Feather Dancer ducked beneath the curtain, nodded to Wink, and took up a guard position by the front door.

"All right, let's begin," Wink said. "Let me remind you that we should all keep our voices down in case any spies sneak up outside."

"I would like to cast my voice first," Wigeon said. She sat up straighter, and her sparse gray hair shimmered with the amber hue of the flames. She wore a coarsely woven white dress that hung over the skeletal frame of her body. The knobs of her elbows resembled knots beneath the fabric. "After our last council meeting, I think it's clear we must do something now, before it's too late. Water Hickory Clan may have disobeyed the council on several occasions, but I believe their actions are correct. We must destroy the Loon Nation."

Wink had expected something like this. Wigeon hated the Loon People. More than one moon ago, she had voted to make war on them for capturing eleven people from Oak Leaf village who had "trespassed" upon gathering grounds claimed by the Loon Nation—grounds that had, in fact, belonged to the Black Falcon Nation for generations.

"I disagree," Matron Black Birch said, and pounded her walking stick on the hearthstones. "Their actions constitute treason. Water Hickory Clan should be Outcast from the nation."

Long Fin said, "Matrons, I think—"

"Birch, be reasonable," Wigeon interrupted. "None of our villages will be safe until we've defeated them once and for all. Can't you see that?"

"Perhaps, we should—," Long Fin tried again.

"What I see, Wigeon, is that your soul is off wandering in the forest somewhere," Birch said. "We would all be better off if we gave the accursed gathering grounds to the Loon People, made peace, and went on with our lives. I don't want my grandchildren dying in a war. Do you?"

Wigeon clenched her fists, as though she longed to strike Birch for calling her crazy. "The situation has escalated to the point that the gathering grounds have become irrelevant. We should—"

"We should have Outcast them a long time ago! You'll recall that *I* voted to do that exact thing. The reason we're in this position now is because the rest of you were cowards."

Wigeon bristled, and Wink held up a hand to halt the argument. "I have new information that I would like to share."

Everyone turned to her.

Long Fin's young face tensed, as though he was upset that no one would let him speak. Inwardly, she sighed. He was proving to be a poor chief, but he'd seen just sixteen winters. She kept praying he would improve. At least he had worn a beautiful cream-colored cape, painted with intricate red and yellow geometric designs. Copper bangles ringed the hem. He looked chiefly, even if he didn't act it.

Wink said, "Chief Long Fin and War Chief Feather Dancer will stand as my witnesses. They were both there during my interrogation."

"Interrogation?" Wigeon arched an eyebrow.

"Yes, three nights ago, I questioned Red Raven. He—"

"That little weasel," Wigeon said. "What could he have told you of any value?"

"Probably a very great deal," Birch defended. "He's Sea Grass' spy."

"Matrons, please let me finish." Wink held up both hands this time, trying to calm the situation. "I had heard, as you had, that Red Raven was the person who found Chief Short Tail's body at Eagle Flute Village. I had him brought to my council chamber to discuss what he'd actually seen, and he admitted to me that he'd gone there to deliver a message to Short Tail."

"What message?" Birch demanded to know. "Was it from Sea Grass?"

Wigeon's lips pressed into a tight line, but she kept silent, waiting for the rest.

"Yes," Wink said, "he was supposed to deliver a message to Short Tail that his next target was Fan Palm Village."

"Another Loon village!" Birch exploded. "Instead of Outcasting them, we should have them all publicly hanged in the plaza!"

"Wait!" Wigeon shouted. "What makes you think Red Raven was telling the truth? He's a well-known, and very skilled, liar."

Wink nodded. "Yes, I know he is, but I think he was telling the truth. War Chief, what did you think?"

Feather Dancer stepped away from the door and into the firelight before he responded, "I have questioned many expert liars, people with more reasons to lie than Red Raven had. I think I am a good judge of such men. It is my opinion, Matrons, that he was telling the truth."

Wink turned to her son. "Chief Long Fin?"

"I think he was too afraid to lie."

Wigeon and Birch glanced at Feather Dancer, suspecting the reason Red Raven had been afraid.

In a low voice, Birch said, "So . . . Sea Grass was going to defy the council again. What do you think of that, Wigeon?"

She crushed the fabric of her white dress in her hands. "It disappoints me. She promised me that Water Hickory Clan would wait for the council's approval before attacking another Loon village."

"It's obvious to anyone with a resident soul that she doesn't care about the council's approval." Birch banged her walking stick again. "We should at least hang *her*."

Priest Teal, who'd been silent through the debate, at last spoke up: "Matrons, this crisis must be resolved. For every single person that we lose, the Loon Nation will lose twenty. Rather than continuing to cast blame, it seems to me you should determine who is the aggrieved party and offer them compensation."

"But Water Hickory Clan will say that they are the aggrieved party," Wigeon pointed out. "The gathering grounds belonged to the Black Falcon Nation, and it was members of their clan who were taken hostage—"

"I think Teal is right," Wink said.

Birch cocked an ear to hear her better. "Are you suggesting a course of action?"

"I am. If Water Hickory Clan wishes to wage its own secret war against the Loon Nation, perhaps the rest of the Black Falcon Nation should take sides."

Silence descended like a granite curtain. The only sounds were the pounding of rain on the roof and the crackling of flames.

Birch gave Wink a sly look. "What makes you think they will agree? They hate us."

Wigeon shook her head as though completely lost. "What are you two gobbling about?"

Long Fin glanced around the circle, examining each woman's expression. When his gaze returned to Wink, he whispered, "Mother, it's too dangerous."

For the first time, Birch glanced at the doorway, then leaned forward to hiss, "He's right. We'll have to send a peace emissary first, and we can't use any of our own people. You know that, don't you? Sea Grass will be keeping track of every warrior we have."

Wink nodded. "I have an outsider in mind."

"An outsider? How can we trust an outsider?" Birch clutched her walking stick in both hands.

"Well, he's an outsider with an interest in the well-being of the Black Falcon Nation."

"Who?" Long Fin asked.

Wink said, "Rockfish."

"Rockfish?" Wigeon blinked, still confused. "Chieftess Sora's husband? What does he have to do with all this?"

"Nothing," Wink said. "Yet."

THE SENSATION OF THE BLANKETS BEING LIFTED, and someone crawling beneath them with her, roused Sora from a deep dreamless sleep.

Flint's hand petted her long black hair. "Forgive me for today. But I couldn't help it, Sora. I needed some time away from that priest." He said the last word like a curse. "I swear he's driving my reflection-soul out of my body."

Sleepily, she opened her eyes. Through a gap in the roof, high above her, tree branches whipped in the wind and stars glittered on a deep blue background. "I was worried about you. Where did you go?"

"Not far. I just walked along the shoreline until some of my anger went away."

A fierce gust of wind thrashed the forest's ancient cypresses, and she drew the worn softness of the blankets up over her bare shoulders. The scent of the lake was powerful tonight, something more than moss and water. In the distance she saw lightning flash. The roar of diving Thunderbirds rumbled across the sky.

Flint looked up at the crude shelter built of poles and rotted thatch that had once formed the walls and roof on the old lodge. "There are holes in this roof big enough for a buzzard to fly through. If it starts to rain again, we'll get soaked."

"By the time we started building shelters, it was dark. We did the best we could." She rolled to her back and yawned.

Flint turned toward Strongheart's shelter five paces away, making certain the priest was asleep. He smoothed his hand over her naked hip, and ran it up her side to stroke her breast. As he squeezed it, he whispered, "I need to talk with you."

She yawned again. "Can't it wait until tomorrow?"

"No."

He bent down to kiss her, and his black hair fell around her like a dark silken curtain. The tenderness of his lips felt as comforting tonight as it had eighteen winters ago.

"What's wrong?"

He rolled on top of her, and she felt his rigid manhood. A tingle shot through her. "I think he's plotting against you."

"Who is?"

Flint lowered his hand and caressed her little manhood. "The priest."

"Why would he do that, Flint?"

"Our people destroyed his village and murdered his family. That's reason enough. His people would consider him a hero if he killed you."

"He hasn't made a single move against me, Flint."

"Of course not. I've been watching him too closely."

He kissed her hard and inserted two fingers into her opening. They moved gently at first, then probed deeper. In less than ten heartbeats, he used his knee to pry her legs apart and slipped his manhood inside her. A groan escaped his throat. In the starlight, she saw the expression of ecstasy on his handsome face. When he began moving, she matched his rhythm.

In her ear, he whispered, "What did he say to you today? After I left."

"Nothing important."

He thrust harder, striking fire along her nerves. "He told you to get rid of me, didn't he? He knows that as soon as I'm gone, he can kill you. There will be no one to stop him."

Warmth began to course through her veins. She said, "Stop talking."

They had loved each other for fifteen winters; he knew her body as well as his own. She locked her legs around his back so that he could force himself deeper. He kept saying, "I love you. I love you, Sora."

When their movements became feverish, she clenched her inner muscles, holding him tight while he lunged against her. Her entire body felt as though it were on fire. The blaze built until she cried out and Flint sagged atop her, panting, "Oh, gods, gods, I need you."

A short distance away, she heard Strongheart's footsteps.

They were headed away, up the shoreline to the north.

Flint's eyes glittered as he watched him.

SEA GRASS HOBBLED ACROSS THE FLOOR OF THE council chamber in the High Matron's House with her faithful guards flanking her. Everyone else was already here, which surprised her. Had Wink asked the other matrons to arrive before Sea Grass, as a subtle way to slight her?

Wink stood in the far corner, speaking with Rockfish. Both had dressed regally, Wink in an azure-colored dress covered with elk ivories, and Rockfish in a knee-length white shirt with black diamonds woven into the hem and around the collar.

Sea Grass' eyes narrowed at the sight of Rockfish. The old gray-haired man had seen more than sixty winters. He had a triangular face with large dark eyes. Most of his muscles had evaporated, leaving loose flaps of skin where bulges had once been. His marriage to Sora had been one of convenience, an alliance of political advantage. They'd married three winters ago, after Flint had set Sora's belongings outside the door and headed home to Oak Leaf Village. The divorce had disgraced Sora. Not only that, she'd loved Flint. She'd made a fool of herself, running after him, begging him to return. It had embarrassed the entire Shadow Rock Clan, much to Water Hickory Clan's delight. As the matron of Oak Leaf Village, Sea Grass had thrown a celebration for Flint when he'd arrived home, and had begun working with his mother to find Flint a new wife. White Fawn was perfect for him: beautiful, clever, and already a skilled warrior. . . .

She grunted as she lowered herself to the south bench and straightened her lavender dress. The torches on the walls cast fluttering light over the sacred masks, making the eyeholes seem alive. Sea Grass silently offered a prayer to the gods, begging them to strike Wink down and allow Water Hickory Clan to rule the nation, as was their due for the men and women they'd lost trying to protect it.

Wigeon glanced at Sea Grass, then ducked her head and twisted her hands in her lap.

Sea Grass' brows lifted. As she looked around, she noticed that Chief Long Fin seemed to be concentrating on the numerous shell rings that adorned his fingers, while Birch stared at Sea Grass with her wrinkled mouth pursed.

"If it won't trouble you, Birch," Sea Grass said, "I'd like to know why your mouth is screwed up like that."

"It wouldn't trouble me to tell you, either, if the high matron hadn't ordered me to keep my tongue to myself today."

"Well, that was a waste of breath on Wink's part. When have you ever kept your tongue from waggling?"

Birch started to say something nasty, but Wink hurried across the floor to intervene, saying, "Matrons, let's not waste our strength arguing when we have more important things to consider."

She stopped in front of the eastern bench and extended a hand to Rockfish. "Chieftess Sora's husband, Rockfish, requested this meeting, so I yield to him." She sat down beside Long Fin, and the elk ivories on her dress clicked musically.

Rockfish folded his arms across his chest. "Matrons, first let me say that my winters in the Black Falcon Nation have been some of the happiest of my life. I hope that my abilities as a Trader have helped the nation, and that the three hundred warriors my people rallied to help defend Blackbird Town have kept more of your young people alive. But . . ." He took a deep breath, and seemed to be struggling with what he wished to say next. "I want your permission to go home."

A soft murmur of voices filled the chamber as people leaned sideways to whisper to each other.

Rockfish continued, "As you know, I have dispatched many search parties trying to find my wife. None has found even a trace of her. It grieves me to say this, but I have been forced to conclude that Sora is dead."

Birch straightened, and her head tottered on the wrinkled stem of her neck. "You are a valued member of the Black Falcon Nation, Rockfish. I ask you to stay. If you go, we will miss you."

"I appreciate your words, Matron, but I am tired. I want to go home and try to Heal my heart."

Blessed gods, what Sora had given Rockfish in prestige he'd given back to her—to the entire Black Falcon Nation—in Trade goods! Every moon another flotilla of canoes appeared, filled to overflowing with rare cherts and mica, silver nuggets, pounded sheets of copper. What would happen if he left?

Sea Grass said, "I hope this will not dissolve the beneficial Trading relationship we have established with your people, Rockfish."

He shook his head, and a lock of gray hair fell over his forehead. "It will not, Matron. I assure you that my people value our Trading relationship as much as you do."

Wink said, "Rockfish, I realize that the past moon has been difficult for you. As the husband of a missing chieftess, your position here has been precarious. But it's been difficult for all of us. If you stay, we will do everything in our power to restore your stature in the nation. Tell us what we may do to convince you?"

He gave her a frail, grateful smile. "You were Sora's lifelong friend, Wink, and a good friend to me. I thank you for your words, but"—he exhaled hard—"home and family are calling to me."

Sea Grass said, "I vote to allow Rockfish to return home to his own people."

"As do I," Birch said.

Widgeon sighed. "I also vote to allow Rockfish to return home."

Long Fin nodded. "I agree."

Wink said, "Then you are free to return home, Rockfish. There is only one thing I ask."

"Yes?"

"I fear that the Black Falcon Nation is still vulnerable. If it is not against the laws of your people, I would ask that you leave your three hundred warriors here for a time longer."

Sea Grass gave Wink an evaluative look, suspecting she was up to something. But what?

Rockfish nodded. "Of course, Wink. Is there anything else?"

"Yes. Remember that you will always be welcome here. Please return as often as you can."

Rockfish bowed to the council, but when he rose, he had a curious expression on his elderly face. "I thank you. Now, there is something else I must tell you."

Sea Grass' ears perked up like a hunting dog with a rabbit in sight. His tone of voice alerted her that he was about to venture into dangerous territory.

"Go on," Wink said.

"My people have already approached me about initiating several new Trading alliances."

"That's none of our concern," Wink said. "Your people may establish alliances with whomever they wish. Just as the Black Falcon People may."

"And do," Birch added.

"Yes, I know that we 'may,' but I want to be forthright with you that my people wish to establish a trading alliance with the Loon Nation. They—"

"You wouldn't!" Sea Grass blurted, and stammered, "That w-would set your people up against ours!"

Rockfish responded, "I don't believe it would, Matron. Currently, the Black Falcon Nation has no alliances of any kind with the Loon Nation."

"Of course we don't! They're animals, and deserve to be treated as such! We—"

"Matron," Rockfish interrupted. "The fact that they are animals may be advantageous. Animals often have furs and meat that are useful to another nation. What we want, in fact, is access to their oyster beds."

Sea Grass stared at him agape. "In that case, I change my vote. I vote not to allow you to go home. Wigeon, what do you say?"

Wigeon, who almost always voted in support of Water Hickory Clan, hesitated, and it infuriated Sea Grass. *Has Wink gotten to you, my old friend?*

In a small, trembling voice, Wigeon said, "My vote stands. High Matron Wink is right. If we begin telling other nations who they may or may not establish trading alliances with, then we can expect them to do the same to us. It is wrong to interfere in the affairs of other nations."

Her eyes narrowed as though she expected Sea Grass to shout at her.

Instead, Sea Grass rose from the bench and announced, "Since I have been outvoted, I assume this council meeting is over."

"It is," Wink said.

Sea Grass waved to her guards and hobbled toward the door. As her guards rushed to pull the curtain back for her, she heard Chief Long Fin whisper, *"You . . . playing with . . . leashed bear, Mother. I pray . . . Skyholder . . ."*

He stopped abruptly, and just before she ducked beneath the curtain, Sea Grass glanced back to see Wink glaring at the boy. Obviously Wink feared that his voice had been too loud.

Sea Grass sternly motioned for her guards to follow her.

13

In the Dream, I weep. . . .

I wrap the cleaned bones of my stillborn child in a blanket and carry them up the steep trail to the top of the Red Hill, where a ladder leans against the ramada. It's awkward, carrying the baby while climbing the ladder to the roof, but I make it, and step out onto the thatch. A scatter of bones already covers the roof. No one allows the bones of animals to touch the ground. Instead, they place them on their roofs where the souls of the animals can keep watch for their new bodies. If animals are killed correctly, with reverence, death is only a temporary thing. Within a few days, Skyholder, the Creator, will send a new body and the soul will rise up from the bones and resume its life.

Humans are born with animal souls. A human soul does not come into the body until a child has seen four or five winters.

I hug the bundle and rock back and forth, begging Skyholder to give me the strength to let this baby go. I know he must be able to watch for his new body, but . . .

Bones clack together as I clutch the baby hard against my breast.

When I start to unfold the blanket, a strange numbing palsy possesses my hands. My fingers won't grasp the fabric.

"Flint?" I call, but no one answers.

He ran away right after the birth, leaving me alone, but I know he's coming back to help me care for the bones. Where is he?

I kneel and place each bone on the roof amid the others. He was so small. His bones resemble tiny white twigs.

I try to rise, to go, but my legs won't work. I can't straighten up. Gasping and struggling, I sob. . . .

Nearby, dry evergreen needles crunch underfoot and a familiar voice soothes, "Can you hear my voice, Sora? Follow it. It will lead you back to Sassafras Lake. I'm here waiting for you. Come back. Everything is all right. Dawn Girl's blue hem is trailing across the forests. Flint is cooking a goose for breakfast."

A hand strokes my hair, and I feel my shadow-soul

seep back into my heavy body. The delicious scent of roasted meat taunts my nostrils. . . .

She opened her eyes and found Strongheart kneeling at her bedside. The yellow starbursts on his buckskin cape looked tan in the light.

"Where was your shadow-soul walking, Chieftess?"

She searched the lodge's dark interior. Streaks of dawn light fell through the gaps in the roof and slanted across her blankets. "On the Red Hill."

"Again?"

She nodded. "I was placing the bones on the roof of the ramada."

Strongheart sank down beside her, and through the door, she could see Flint's distinct silhouette crouched before a goose that had been skewered on a stick and propped near the flames. As he turned it so the other side would cook, hot fat dripped onto the fire and filled the air with a wonderful aroma.

"Was Flint there this time?" Strongheart asked.

"No. But he wasn't there in reality either; why do you think he'd suddenly appear in my dreams?"

Strongheart just smiled and studied the movements of her hands on her blanket. She looked down. She hadn't realized that her thumbs were tapping out an irregular staccato. "What happened after you placed the bones on the roof?"

"I walked home."

"Was Flint there when you arrived?"

"No. He stayed gone for several days."

She had never been the same. For moons afterward, she'd heard that little boy calling to her. She had prayed constantly that a pregnant woman would walk past the Red Hill and her little boy's soul would slip into the woman's womb and find a new body waiting for him. To this day, not a single night went by that she didn't feel her son searching for her in her dreams.

Wink's voice penetrated her memories: *Oh, Sora, all women worry about the souls of children they've lost. Don't think you're going to get over it. You won't. Not ever.*

"Did you forgive Flint for leaving you alone?" Strongheart asked.

"Of course I did. I was always the stronger of the two of us. He just couldn't stand it."

She looked past Strongheart to Flint, and found him staring straight into her eyes. Her souls ached for him. He had never had the strength to face anything truly difficult. She had always been his shield against the world.

Strongheart touched her hand where it lay on the blanket. "Sora, do you know the story of the three brothers and the pitying wives?"

She blinked and looked back at him. "No. I don't think so."

"It's a very popular story among my people." He pulled his hand away, as though to withdraw the comfort he'd been giving. "Three brothers all married within a moon of each other. Both their father and their grandfather had been adulterers, so the brothers saw nothing wrong with it. The first time the eldest brother came home smelling of another woman, his wife told him if it ever happened again, she would divorce him. She was the only one to save her husband from his destructive family. The other wives blamed themselves and so pitied their husbands that they coddled them like overprotective mothers, and pleaded with them to stay home. One brother was run over by a herd of buffalo on the way to a married woman's house. The last brother died when he was lanced through the heart by the enraged father of a little girl."

Sora stared at him. "Are you saying that I am like the two pitying wives?"

"I'm saying that it is the duty of every adult woman to rid herself of the sort of pity that contributes to the destruction of the man she loves."

For an instant, she did not know what to say. His voice had no anger in it, no reproach; it was just a realistic statement about life.

When, after several heartbeats, she hadn't answered, he added, "The wrong kind of pity frees the evil Spirits that lurk inside human beings, Sora. It can be very dangerous."

He rose and ducked out of the old lodge.

Flint called, "Is she all right?"

"Yes," Strongheart answered. "She's awake. How's the goose coming?"

"Almost ready."

Sora sat up and reached for her sky blue dress. When the wind blew, the scents of moldering wood and damp vines seeped from the old lodge like a pall. Every time she inhaled, she had the urge to cough. She slipped her dress over her head, laced on her sandals, and combed her hair before ducking outside into the cool morning.

Birds crowded the trees around the lake, hopping from branch to branch, uttering a cacophony of chirps and caws. The pearlescent glow of sunrise reflecting off the water flickered in the veils of hanging moss near the shore.

She walked out into the deep forest shadows to empty her night water.

As she walked back, she felt unusually tired. She always did after the Red Hill dream. It was as though, even now, trying to care for her baby's bones alone took all of her strength.

Flint and Strongheart stood around the fire, talking quietly. Against the predawn gleam of the lake, their bodies resembled tall dark pillars.

"Would you like a cup of tea?" Strongheart asked. "It's made from dried pitch apples."

"Where did you find dried pitch apples?"

"In a sealed pot in Juggler's old house." He dipped up a cupful and handed it to her.

The sweet tangy fragrance of apples rose with the steam.

Flint reached out to pet her hair. "What was your bad dream about?"

"I—I don't recall," she answered with a shrug. "I rarely recall the dreams that wake me."

She had never told him about her recurring Red Hill dream. He would take it as an accusation, and she couldn't bear to see that hateful expression on his handsome face.

Flint said, "Did you tell Strongheart about it?" and threw a quick, resentful glance at the priest.

"Flint, if I don't remember it how could I tell Strongheart or anyone else?"

Flint's icy stare riveted on Strongheart, but Strongheart just sipped his cup of tea, meeting Flint's gaze with equanimity.

As though to demonstrate he'd heard part of the conversation, Flint said, "What was that lecture you were giving on pity, Strongheart?"

Strongheart knelt before the tea pot to refill his cup. "I was telling the chieftess that shielding another's weaknesses is good, except when it encourages them to destroy themselves."

"Shielding another's weaknesses," Flint said with mock thoughtfulness. "Like I did for you, Sora?"

He was trying to pick a fight. Perhaps he'd heard her say that she'd always been the stronger of the two of them. How much more had he heard? Her Red Hill dream? A shiver ran across her shoulders.

"Yes," she answered straightforwardly. And to change the subject, she asked, "That goose smells delicious. Who shot it?"

Flint's mouth pressed into a tight line. He knew

what she was doing. He gestured to Strongheart. "The priest netted it."

Sora's brows lifted in admiration. "Netting a goose is a feat of magic."

"Not really," he said. "I used to live here. I know every place on the lake where they sleep. It's a simple matter to drop a net over one or two if you're a fair hunter."

As Mother Sun neared waking, a pink bubble of light swelled on the eastern horizon and turned the bellies of the drifting Cloud People a rose color.

Sullenly, Flint said, "If Strongheart is right that the wrong kind of pity looses the evil Spirits that live inside a person, perhaps that's where the Midnight Fox came from." When Sora visibly lost color, Flint continued, "My pity for you."

"Did you pity her?" Strongheart inquired.

"Of course I did. She was a lonely little girl, a goddess descended directly from our legendary hero Black Falcon. The entire nation expected glorious things from her. No one could have lived up to those expectations."

"Is that why you married her? You felt sorry for her?"

Flint folded his arms across his chest. "No, Priest. I loved her. I still love her."

Sora longed to run to him, to comfort him, as she had always done when he told her he loved her, but this time, she didn't move. The story of the pitying wives made her wonder *why* she longed to do that.

The realization was like a club swung into her belly. *Blessed gods, I pity him for loving me.*

Flint, clearly upset that she hadn't responded as he'd expected her to, tossed the dregs of his tea into the fire and stalked away.

Strongheart said, "We should eat before the goose overcooks and dries out."

Faintly, she heard herself say, "Yes."

While Strongheart cut up the goose and placed the meat into bowls, her eyes followed Flint up the trail and out into the forest. "He seems to walk away in anger a good deal of late."

Strongheart handed her a bowl of steaming goose, and extended a hand. "Let's go over to that fallen log and sit down while we eat."

They carried their bowls and tea cups to the log. When they were sitting with their bowls in their laps looking out over the water, he asked, "Are you all right?"

"I just . . . I realized something for the first time."

Strongheart took a bite of his goose, chewed, and swallowed before softly saying, "Do you want to tell me about it?"

She shook her head, as if to deny her own revelation. "I have always pitied Flint for loving me. That's why every time he's ever told me he loves me I've felt the urge to run into his arms to pet and comfort him."

Strongheart looked at her from the corner of his eye. "That's not unusual. Most women do that."

She jerked around to stare at him. "Why?"

"It's complicated to explain."

As she tore off a piece of meat with her teeth, she said, "Try."

He wiped his greasy mouth on his sleeve. "It happens because women have male shadow-souls."

"Male shadow-souls? What does that mean?"

"It means there's a man who lives inside you."

"Really," she said, skeptical. "I don't think I know him."

"Oh, I think you do. He is your strength and daring. It's his voice that tells you 'of course you can do it,' when logic says 'it's impossible.' But his soul can also be very harmful. Whenever a woman is alone, it's the male shadow-soul that tells her she's lonely and ugly and a disappointment to everyone who loves her. Unfortunately, women tend to project their shadow-souls onto the real men in their lives."

Sora's face slackened. "So it's my shadow-soul telling me that anyone who loves me should be pitied?"

"Yes, and you obviously believe him."

She turned to gaze out at the lake while she thought about it. In the distance, sunlight glimmered from the backs of ducks as they sailed down toward the green water.

"I do believe him," she whispered.

"Then you're not grateful for love, you're ashamed that you've duped a man into feeling that way. Is that it?"

Her mouth fell open. *Was* that it?

"What makes this even more difficult," he said, "is that men have female shadow-souls."

She straightened. "You have a female soul inside you?"

"I do."

Half in jest, she asked, "And what does she say to you when you're alone?"

Strongheart smiled down at his bowl and ate another piece of goose. "Mostly that I'm weak and stupid, and I'll never be a success at anything."

"Well, she's certainly wrong about that. You're the greatest Healer in our world."

"She doesn't think so. She thinks I'm a fraud."

Sora gave him a disbelieving look. The brightening light shone on the arch of his hooked nose and the high curves of his cheeks. If she did not look into his eyes, he appeared very young, younger than his twenty-three winters, but his eyes contradicted every other physical observation. They held a calm centuries deep. Once caught by his gaze, it was hard to look away. She always felt that if she just kept looking, she would find an answer for every question she had ever asked.

She frowned. "Then even if a wife isn't telling her husband that he's weak and stupid and a failure, he thinks she is? Because he hears his own shadow-soul's voice coming out of her mouth?"

Strongheart nodded. "Both male and the female shadow-souls are monstrously clever at deception. They want the human being to believe the words are coming from outside. It gives them more power."

Sora pulled off another strip of meat and ate it. "I wonder how marriages survive."

He just tilted his head as though it were a mystery to him as well.

Around the edge of the lake, the cypress' trunks still held the azure deeps of night, but a pale yellow gleam painted the branches and the backs of the waterfowl that paddled the water.

She cast a sideways glance at Strongheart. Two upright lines had formed between his brows. He seemed to be concentrating on finishing his breakfast. She wondered what it was about the combination of his deep gentle voice and his luminous eyes that drew her so powerfully. Over the past quarter moon, he had carved out his own space inside her, leaving her feeling hollow and lonely whenever he was away.

Strongheart set his empty bowl on the log between them and retrieved his tea cup to sip it. "Do you think it's possible that Flint was right?"

"Hmm?" she said in confusion. "About what?"

"That his pity for you is what loosed the Midnight Fox?"

"No," she said too quickly. "The Midnight Fox first appeared to me when I'd seen seven winters, long before I met Flint."

He swirled his tea in his cup before taking a long drink.

"What's wrong, Priest?"

"You chose not to answer my question."

Her gaze darted around the camp. "I did?"

"I asked if his pity had loosed the Fox, not created it."

"Oh . . . well, I—I don't know how to answer that. It's something I've never thought of. I don't think it's likely, though. Do you?"

He smiled, and pointed to a large fish that leaped out of the water. She looked just in time to see it splash down and send a spray over a nearby duck that squawked and shook its feathers.

She took another bite of succulent goose, and juice dribbled down her chin. As she wiped it away, she said, "Now you're the one who's not answering questions. It frightens me."

He clutched his tea cup and looked down at his fingers for a long moment—shiny with grease, she saw, and in the growing sunlight, splotched with soot. "I suspect you might be a good deal more frightened if I did."

As though to forestall the discussion, he rose to his feet and extended a hand to her. "Eat that last bite and come walk with me."

She gobbled down her goose, set her bowl down, and took his hand. He helped her up, then released her fingers and backed away slightly, as though shocked by his own reaction to touching her.

He smiled self-consciously and said, "Let's take the northern trail around the lake. It's very pretty this time of season." He started up the same trail that Flint had taken, carrying his half-full tea cup with him.

Sora followed a few steps behind him. "Where are we going?"

"To the opposite side of the lake. There's a cave there."

They slowly walked around an inlet where fish tails flipped the surface of the water.

Sora said, "Tell me about Juggler. Was he a great Healer?"

"Yes, though many considered him to be a witch."

"Why? Was he evil?"

He looked over his shoulder and said, "Evil is an amorphous thing. Juggler used Spirit plants to Heal many people, but he also used them to poison his enemies, who were all very wicked, or so he told me."

"Naturally," she said. "How did he survive the accusations of witchcraft?"

"First, he was a doddering elder with an idiotic smile. No one who met him could believe he was a witch. Second, he denied the accusations, and no one could ever prove he'd done anything wrong. Which was exactly what he'd counted on."

"Then he was a witch?"

Strongheart glanced back at her, and leaf shadows danced over his short, irregularly cut black hair. "It doesn't matter. At least, not to me. After my parents died, he took me in. He was my entire world. He—"

"He trained you as a witch?"

His eyes sparkled. "Do you think I'm a witch?"

"It doesn't matter," she mimicked. "Not to me. So long as you can cure me."

His expression turned serious. He didn't answer for a time, then he murmured, "I can, Sora. I give you my oath, but I need your help."

"Just tell me what to do. I'll do anything you ask."

After a moment, he said, "Will you?"

"Yes, of course. Why wouldn't I?"

He remained silent.

She said, "Do you think I'm *not* helping you?"

As he held aside a low-hanging branch and gestured for her to walk out front, he said, "On occasion you work against me."

She walked forward and stopped less than a hand's breadth away to look up at him. "I don't do it on purpose."

"I know."

Their gazes held, and a pained longing filled her. She wished she'd never met him, never known what it was to feel his touch or know the deep sound of his voice.

Gently, he asked, "What do you want to say to me?"

She opened her mouth, hesitated . . . and walked up the trail.

What could she say that wouldn't force him into a corner? After twenty heartbeats, she called, "You told me once that your parents had been killed by the Lily People when you'd seen nine winters."

"Yes. My parents had gone north to attend the marriage of my uncle. They were ambushed on the trail. I was at home with my grandmother. I didn't find out they'd been killed for almost a moon."

"I don't understand why you came to live with Juggler. Among my people, one of your relatives would have adopted you."

"Eventually that's what happened. But not at first."

"Why not? In the Black Falcon Nation it would have been inconceivable to allow a recently orphaned child to be taken to a total stranger."

"I was . . ." He paused as though remembering, and she heard him take a drink from his tea cup. "A difficult child. My relatives were frightened by me."

She walked into a patch of warm sunlight and stopped. He stayed a full two paces away. "Did you have Spirit Powers even then?"

"Oh, yes. They came to me at three or four winters. My mother used to say that every rock and bird in the sky was my Spirit Helper."

"But you must have done something to make your relatives fear you."

He didn't respond for a long time; then finally he answered, "I did. I killed a boy."

The forest seemed go silent around them. Even the wind stilled. The mossy scent of the lake grew stronger.

In a hushed voice, she asked, "What happened?"

He gestured uncertainly with his free hand. "We were playing and he shoved me. I landed so hard it knocked the wind out of me. When I could breathe again, I pointed at him and cursed him."

"And?"

"He dropped as though I'd hit him in the head with a war club. He was dead. The other children ran away screaming. After that, no one felt safe around me."

"How old were you?"

"I'd seen five winters."

Blessed Spirits, is it possible that such a young child could have gathered enough Power to kill?

"Do you think you killed him?"

His brows drew down over his nose. "Everyone believed that I'd done it. After my parents died it was my grandmother's excuse to be rid of me. She stuffed my clothes in my pack and had me escorted here, to Sassafras Lake, to 'study' with Juggler. I think she genuinely hoped he could teach me to control my Spirit Powers. I did try very hard to learn from him."

The love in his voice touched her. "He must have been like a father to you."

"Yes. Or at least he was my best friend."

His gaze drifted away from her and out to the sunlit trees, where long beards of hanging moss swayed. His shadow-soul seemed to be walking trails from long ago, not all of them pleasant.

"Why did you decide to leave him and return to Eagle Flute Village?"

"I didn't decide to leave him." He braced a hand on a nearby palm trunk; his sleeve fell down, revealing the beautiful tattoos that covered his arm. Red and azure, the interconnected bands of human eyes seemed to be staring straight at her. "He threw me out, told me to go home. For moons I secreted myself in caves around Sassafras Lake, praying he would change his mind and come looking for me. Yesterday when we found his lodge empty and I knew he must be dead . . ." He grimaced at his tea cup. "It's the first time I've known for certain that he would never change his mind. I—I always thought he would, some day, send for me."

Sora put a hand on his shoulder and squeezed gently. "It must have been difficult, losing your parents, then your family, and finally the one person you thought loved you."

Strongheart started to place his hand over hers, but stopped midway with his fingers hovering above hers. He grasped his tea cup instead. "He did love me, Chieftess. That's why he made me go home. I just didn't understand it at the time. He'd taught me everything he could. I needed to face the world. I wouldn't have done it if he hadn't forced me to."

"How long had you been with him?"

"Three winters."

"Then you were twelve winters old. That hardly seems old enough to face the world, Priest."

She walked around him and continued up the trail. The velvet touch of the wind stirred the massive beech and oak branches that canopied the trail, scenting the air with a pungent fragrance. She breathed it in. As the day warmed, swarms of insects climbed from their hiding places and created great glittering veils in the sunlit depths of the forest. As she slowed to veer around a fallen tree that blocked the trail, she heard Strongheart's soft steps come up behind her. Just as she started to step into the brush, he grabbed her arm, and she heard his tea cup thunk on the ground.

"Wh—"

She only got out part of the word before his hand clamped over her mouth, and he leaned down to whisper, "Be very quiet. Look through the berry vines." He removed his hand and pointed.

At first she saw nothing but the dense tangle of vines; then one of the men moved. He stepped to the left and she could see him. It was Flint. His mouth was moving as though he was talking to someone she couldn't see.

Sora glanced up at Strongheart and noticed that his gaze was not on Flint, but on the person Flint spoke with. He was much taller than she. He could probably see both men. He looked down at her and mouthed the words, "Get down."

They both eased to the ground and stretched out on their bellies in the trail. When she started to ask a question, he placed his fingers against her lips and shook his head.

It didn't take long, perhaps another thirty heartbeats, for the two men to part. Flint walked off in the direction of camp. The unknown man headed south at a trot, as though in a hurry to leave.

Sora waited until Flint had walked far out of sight before she murmured, "Who was the other man? Did you know him?"

Strongheart shook his head. "But the fine cloth he wore definitely marked him as a member of the Black Falcon Nation."

"Could you see him clearly? What did he look like?"

"He was a short with hunched shoulders and had rotted front teeth."

Like a knife had been thrust into her belly, she felt the stab of recognition. But . . . it couldn't be . . . Stammering, she asked, "D-did his nose twitch constantly? Like a trapped rat's?"

Strongheart nodded. "Yes, do you know him?"

For no apparent reason, her voice shook when she responded, "It might have been Red Raven."

"Who is he?"

"Sea Grass' spy."

"Is she Water Hickory Clan?"

"Yes, she's the matron of Oak Leaf Village. Flint's home village. Sea Grass was Skinner's mother."

Strongheart moved closer to her to whisper, "How did Red Raven know where to find Flint?"

A sharp pain stabbed right behind her eyes. She rubbed her forehead. "Flint told him?"

Strongheart reached out, took her hand, and pulled it away from her forehead. He whispered, "We should go."

He picked up his cracked cup and dusted it off as he got to his feet. Taking her hand, he silently led her up the trail through the dappled shadows, heading away from camp.

14

WINK WALKED AROUND THE EDGES OF THE BROAD plaza, glanced at the chunkey game playing out on the field, and went straight for the War Chief's Mound with her guard close at her heels. Clearwing's head kept turning to take in the game, and she could tell he wished he were out there practicing with the other warriors.

People crowded the edges of the field, their eyes alight, hissing when the calls went against them, cheering when their clan won. They watched Wink pass, but no one dared to speak with her.

As she strode past the huge cooking pots that smelled of opossum and fresh spring herbs, her empty stomach knotted. She had not been eating well, or sleeping well, for that matter—and there was no relief in sight. . . .

Cheers went up, and from the corner of her eye she saw the chunkey stone, round and about the width of her hand, rolling like the wind for the far end of the field. Warriors raced after it. When they hit the casting line, they launched their spears. Clearwing made a deep-throated sound of excitement, and Wink stopped long enough to allow him to see who scored. Water Hickory Clan played against Shadow Rock Clan today. Whoever hit the stone earned two points. Whoever's spear landed closest to the stone earned one point. If this were a real chunkey game, the opposing teams would be playing for a deadly serious reason, perhaps to break a tie vote in the Council of Elders, which would determine whether or not they went to war or established a new alliance with an enemy nation.

Clearwing hissed and waved a hand when Water Hickory Clan scored the point.

Wink said, "They always have superior players."

"That's because they practice constantly, Matron. We are too busy planting and harvesting our fields to keep our skills honed." He was a medium-sized man with a square face and dark serious eyes. He wore a red knee-length warshirt.

"Yes," she replied absently, and continued toward Feather Dancer's mound. "Regrettable." Her thoughts were on other things—things no one but she and Feather Dancer knew.

To the north, in front of her, stood the War Chief's Mound. Over the past three winters they'd undertaken several mound-building projects, both here and elsewhere in Black Falcon country, that would have been impossible before Sora's marriage to Rockfish. The wealth generated by that Trade relationship had given them stunning new abilities. As they raised mounds so that Grandmother Earth could touch fingertips with her daughter, Mother Sun, their lives improved dramatically. It was as though the gods saw and approved. The bright fabrics, elaborate copper and silver jewelry, and glittering shell beads were testaments to a time of riches beyond anyone's belief.

It also made them targets. Every greedy nation on earth wanted some of their wealth—that was the essence of the dispute with the Loon Nation over the gathering grounds.

As she marched up the steps of the War Chief's Mound, her green dress blew around her legs, revealing the flashing copper anklets she wore.

She stepped off onto the mound top, and Feather Dancer ducked beneath his door curtain and bowed to her. Small in comparison to the other elite buildings in Blackbird Town, the War Chief's House was fifteen paces square and constructed of massive upright cypress logs. The roof soared four times the height of a man.

"War Chief," she greeted, "is everything ready?"

"Yes, Matron." But his wary eyes scanned the mound and the plaza below.

Wink turned to Clearwing. "Warrior, while I am here, the war chief will guard me. I have another duty for you."

Clearwing blinked as though confused; he generally

stood right outside Feather Dancer's door, but he said, "Yes, Matron?"

"Find Tern. Tell her I wish to speak with her tonight, then return as soon as you can."

"Tern? Elder Bittern's daughter?"

"Yes."

"Very well, Matron." He trotted away.

Feather Dancer held the door curtain aside for her, and she ducked into the dim firelit house. The elderly man on the far side rose to his feet and dipped his head to acknowledge her. At least fifty winters old, he had a full head of dark gray hair and a deeply wrinkled face.

She nodded in response, but waited for Feather Dancer to enter before she proceeded.

In a low voice, Feather Dancer said, "High Matron, this is Raider. He comes as emissary from Chief Sand Conch, high chief of the Loon Council."

Wink strode across the floor to greet him, and to her surprise he gracefully dropped to his knees and kissed her sandals, saying, "I understand, High Matron, that this is a sign of respect among your people."

"Yes, it is. I appreciate the gesture, but it was not necessary, Raider. Please rise."

He grunted as he got to his feet and seemed to be favoring his right hip. The rapid two-day trip from the Loon Nation had apparently left it aching.

Wink held out a hand to the sitting mats spread around the fire in the center of the Feather Dancer's house. "Please, sit and have some tea. I'm sure you had a difficult journey."

"Yes, it seems my aging body is no longer well-suited to skulking through the underbrush in the Black Falcon Nation."

Feather Dancer crouched and dipped up two cups of tea from the pot resting on the hearthstones. As he handed one to her, then one to Raider, he said, "Matron, do you wish me to remain, or stand outside the door?"

"Remain, War Chief. I may need your advice."

Feather Dancer nodded, but he remained standing while she and Raider settled onto mats. No one was certain what to expect, least of all Wink. She was in unknown waters, floundering for a shore she could not even see, let alone imagine the coastline of.

"High Matron," Raider said in a mild elderly voice, "Chief Sand Conch wishes me to tell you that he received your message and looks forward to the arrival of your peace emissary. He is grateful that you wish to end the war, but he does not understand. If you did not wish a war, why did you attack one of our villages, burn it to the ground, and hunt down every fleeing survivor you could find? These do not sound like the actions of a woman seeking peace."

Wink gave him a short nod. "The attack was not under my orders, Raider; in fact it went against the orders of our Council of Elders. The attack was undertaken strictly by the Water Hickory Clan. They alone are responsible."

His brows lifted. "I see. And what should we tell our people? That the Black Falcon Council of Elders cannot control its own clans?"

Feather Dancer took a step forward, prepared to defend her against the insult, but Wink held up a hand. "No, War Chief, Raider's question is fair."

Raider tipped his head in gratitude, but said, "High Matron, would it be possible to have the war chief guard the door? I would hate to have him crush my skull out of some reflex before we'd finished our discussion."

Wink nodded to Feather Dancer, and he went to stand by the door.

She looked Raider over more carefully. Chief Sand Conch had chosen his messenger well. The man's age and mild manner smoothed over the effect of his lightning-charged words.

"Let us speak straightly, Raider."

"Of course, High Matron."

She set her untouched tea cup on the hearthstones. "I'm not sure we can control the Water Hickory Clan. I heard only a few days ago that the new clan matron had ordered her warriors to attack Fan Palm Village."

Raider jerked forward with his eyes wide. "When?"

"I don't know. The death of Chief Short Tail, who led the attack on Eagle Flute Village, will delay Sea Grass, but she'll select a new leader very soon. I believe the attack is inevitable."

He squeezed his eyes closed. It took him a few moments to collect himself. Finally, he asked, "Why do you tell me this?"

Wink waited until he opened his eyes before she said, "Because I need your help to stop it."

"My help? I don't understand."

"The Council of Elders voted not to Outcast Water Hickory Clan from the Black Falcon Nation—it is more afraid of civil war than of war with the Loon Nation—but I will not stand by and watch more innocent people murdered."

By the door, Feather Dancer shifted positions, spreading his feet. Raider cocked his head curiously. "What are you proposing?"

"An alliance."

Behind his eyes, she could see his souls start to walk down the same paths hers had been walking for a quarter moon. "Between what parties, High Matron?"

"There is only one clan I *can* control. My own."

Raider peered at her through narrowed eyes for so long that she had to clamp her hands to keep them from fidgeting. Finally, he asked, "What will your people say about this?"

"They will say that I have set Shadow Rock Clan up against Water Hickory Clan. They will accuse me of betraying the Black Falcon Nation. They will say I have initiated civil war."

"And afterward?" he asked in a mild voice. "Will you continue as high matron of the Black Falcon Nation?"

What he meant was would they kill her for it.

She tilted her head. "That remains to be seen."

Raider drank his tea.

Wink looked at Feather Dancer. His face showed no emotion at all, though he must be wondering why she had not briefed him on this plan before the meeting.

The truth was she couldn't trust anyone with this information. If a breath of it got out and made it to Sea Grass . . .

Thank the gods Rockfish agreed to leave his three hundred warriors here. I only pray that's enough.

Wink lifted her chin. "My emissary, Rockfish, has orders that he and his party are to remain in Fan Palm Village as your hostages until you willingly release them. If you allow it, Rockfish will act as my voice in any negotiations between our peoples."

Raider fingered his cup. "You trust him that much?"

"He is the husband of our missing chieftess. I trust him that much."

Raider frowned at the fire for a time. He seemed to be trying to decide what could be safely said. Finally, he looked back at Wink. "Very well, High Matron, if you are willing to risk your life and your clan, we agree to consider your proposal. In exchange, may I give you some information about the Water Hickory Clan. It is, I believe, information you are unaware of."

Anxiety knotted in her belly. She glanced at Feather Dancer and noticed that he'd taken a step forward. "Please."

"Almost one moon ago, your high chieftess came to Eagle Flute Village, supposedly to negotiate with our chief, Blue Bow, for the release of eleven hostages we were holding."

"Yes, Sora never appeared. I know, and I deeply regret any misunderstandings—"

"If I am not mistaken, the version of the story you know came from Chief Blue Bow."

She stared at him. On the night he died, Blue Bow had told Long Fin that Sora left camp with Walking Bird, but before they arrived, she had disappeared into the trees. His scouts had tried to track her, but she was too shrewd for them. They never saw Sora again. Walking Bird entered the village alone, told Blue Bow that he was a willing hostage sent by Sora as a promise that she would appear within five days. When she didn't, they killed Walking Bird.

Where did she go? White Fawn was killed during that crucial time period.

"Most of my version came from Blue Bow. Why?"

"Chief Blue Bow was a cautious man. Fearing he might need the details later, for leverage, he did not tell your son the whole truth."

"Does it matter now?"

"It may."

Feather Dancer took two steps forward, and Wink nodded to him to come all the way. He'd been there, after all, with a party of thirty warriors. Sora had ordered Feather Dancer to camp outside Eagle Flute Village while she and Walking Bird went in to see Chief Blue Bow alone. Feather Dancer had never forgiven himself for obeying that order.

"What happened?" Feather Dancer crouched on the opposite side of the fire, and the thick scars that wormed across his face gleamed.

Raider said, "Walking Bird tried to negotiate for the release of the hostages himself. He said that you, personally, High Matron, had authorized him to deal with the Loon Nation."

Wink's lips parted. "I did no such thing! The council authorized Sora, and only Sora, to negotiate with Blue Bow."

Raider lifted a shoulder. "Walking Bird offered us great wealth to release the hostages. When Blue Bow refused and insisted upon seeing Chieftess Sora, Walking Bird flatly stated that she was not coming, and told Chief Blue Bow that he would have to deal with him or face the wrath of Water Hickory Clan." Raider smoothed his fingers over the sides of his cup, tracing the designs. "I have always wondered how he knew the chieftess wasn't coming. I thought, perhaps, you might wonder about that as well."

Wink exchanged a look with Feather Dancer. The truth seemed to dawn on him before it did on her; he slowly rose to his feet, drew his stiletto from his belt, and headed for the door.

"Feather Dancer, wait!" she called.

He stopped, but didn't turn around, and she could see his muscles bulging through his warshirt. He'd started to shake with rage.

"Not now," she ordered in a low voice. "Soon, I promise, but this is not the time."

It took a few moments before he again took up his position by the door.

Raider gave Wink a small smile. "I hope that I have been helpful."

"You have." She stood up. "Now, for both our sakes, you should get out of Blackbird Town as soon as possible, but it will be easier under the cover of darkness. I recommend you remain here until nightfall. Is that acceptable?"

"Yes, if I am not a burden."

Wink gestured to Feather Dancer. "War Chief, make certain that our guest is *very* comfortable."

Feather Dancer inclined his head. "Of course, Matron."

Wink strode for the doorway with her heart pounding in her throat. Feather Dancer held aside the curtain for her. Their gazes barely touched before she ducked out into the warm sunlight . . . but it was enough.

In that brief moment, they sealed a bargain.

15

SORA SAT JUST OUTSIDE THE CAVE WHERE STRONG-heart had played as a child. Enormous sassafras trees and water oaks had grown up in front of the small opening, almost blocking it. As she leaned down to peer inside, a damp earthy fragrance breathed out. It was absolutely black inside. "Were you happy here?"

Strongheart stood four paces away, near the lakeshore, and seemed to be studying the late-afternoon light that lay like sheets of pounded copper between the distant cypresses.

"Sometimes." He picked up a pebble and tossed it into the water. "Toward the end, I only came here after Juggler had shouted at me."

"It sounds as though he grew cranky in his old age."

"No, it wasn't age; it was me. I knew he wanted me to go home, but the more he tried to shove me away, the harder I clung to him like a bug to a sinking canoe."

Her gaze drifted across the sunlit water to the opposite shore, and despair filtered through her. All day long she'd been second-guessing herself. She hadn't actually seen the man Flint spoke to; maybe it wasn't Red Raven. There must be a thousand men in the world that fit Strongheart's description. However, if it had been Red Raven the ramifications were staggering. "We should get back to camp."

"Are you sure?"

She massaged her aching temples. "Maybe it wasn't Red Raven. I should give Flint the chance to explain."

Me and the pitying wives.

But at her first step, he held out a hand—a sort of weightless, noiseless gesture, almost ghostlike. "Before we return, I need to know about White Fawn," he said.

"White Fawn?"

"You said you thought you may have killed her. I need to know why you think that."

"I—I'm not sure I know why."

A breath of wind caught his shirtsleeve and flapped it against his side like the tapping of fingers upon a door. "You did know. What changed your mind?"

She gestured awkwardly. "Too many pieces don't fit."

"What are the pieces?"

"They're glimpses . . . faces. Warriors scouting the forest . . . a beautiful woman being carried on a litter . . .

I must have been there, or I wouldn't know what she looked like, would I? And if I was there . . ."

I killed her.

"Tell me what she looked like?"

Sora heaved a sigh and closed her eyes, seeing the woman again. "She was young, maybe fifteen winters, with long black hair and a thin pointed face. Pretty." She reached up to touch her own ears. "Her pounded copper earrings had been twisted into spirals. I—I was there. I must have been."

Strongheart's brown eyes had fixed on her, depthless and unblinking, as though seeing into the past.

"Being there," he said, "doesn't mean you killed her. It means you were there. Providing the woman you saw was White Fawn. What makes you think it was?"

"Well," she said in a rush of breath, "who else could it have been?"

"Had you ever seen her before?"

"No."

"Then it could have been any bridal procession."

She shook her head fiercely. "No, her father said he saw me in the forest the night she died. I must have done it."

Her emotion never touched the milky stillness of his calm. He extended a hand to the sandy shore. "Sit with me. Let's start from the beginning."

She walked over and dropped to the sand.

As Mother Sun descended into the western underworld, her gleam reflected from the lake with blinding intensity. She had to shield her eyes with her hand to watch Strongheart sit down cross-legged beside her.

"The beginning," he said.

"I don't know where the beginning is." She suddenly felt very old and tired.

"Then let me start. . . . Flint told me that your party camped outside Eagle Flute Village. You told Feather Dancer you were going in with just one guard, Walking Bird. But you sent Walking Bird in alone and you vanished into the trees. Do you recall that?"

She shook her head. "Some of it. I did order Feather Dancer to camp just outside your village and told him I would be going in with only one guard, Walking Bird."

"That was very dangerous. Why did you do it?"

"Walking Bird and I had discussed it the night before over dinner. We agreed that it would be a gesture of goodwill if just the two of us went in, alone and unarmed."

"Did you walk away into the trees?"

Through a taut exhalation, she answered, "Strongheart, I don't even remember walking away from our camp that morning."

"Feather Dancer told me that when you returned five days later you told him a Loon warrior had tried to kill you the instant you set foot in Eagle Flute Village. To protect you, Walking Bird had leaped in front of you and taken the arrow himself. He was dead."

"Feather Dancer wouldn't lie about that. I just don't recall saying it."

He touched her hand. "Look at me."

She lifted her head.

Gently, he said, "You and I both know that's not how it happened. Walking Bird entered Eagle Flute Village alone and remained there for five days, trying to negotiate the release of the hostages. Chief Blue Bow considered it insulting to have to deal with a lowly warrior. He refused to negotiate the release with Walking Bird, preferring to wait for you. When you never arrived, Blue Bow ordered him killed."

It had never occurred to her that Walking Bird would have tried to negotiate the release himself, but of course he would have. That was their mission, the reason they'd gone to Eagle Flute Village. With or without her, he knew what had to be done.

"If I didn't go north to kill White Fawn, where was I? These are the pieces that *do* fit. Eagle Flute Village was two days away from the bridal procession. I must have gone north, killed her, and returned to our camp outside of Eagle Flute Village."

He didn't move, as though he feared any extraneous gestures would distract her. "What did Flint tell you about the days before White Fawn's murder? He and War Chief Skinner went out to meet the bridal procession. Then what happened?"

"He told me that by the time they arrived, White Fawn was dead. Her family thought she'd been poisoned. It was only later that he discovered I'd been missing when White Fawn was killed."

"What made Flint believe you'd killed her?"

For a time, it hurt too much to speak. "He said he and

Skinner weren't sure which trail the bridal procession was going to take. The barbarian Lily People had been raiding the borders of their territory; the procession had to be careful. He and Skinner took two different trails, hoping to catch the procession and lead them to Big Cypress Spring, where they would have warriors waiting to escort them into Oak Leaf Village. They promised to meet up at Big Cypress Spring. Two days later, they did, but neither had seen the procession. Frantic, they began searching the lesser, little-used trails."

"They found the procession."

"Yes, at nightfall. Everyone was weeping and tearing at their clothing. White Fawn's father said he thought he'd glimpsed a strange woman out in the trees the night his daughter died. He thought it was a Forest Spirit. Skinner said—and Flint agreed—that I was the only woman who would want White Fawn dead. That's when he decided he had to find someone to help me. To Heal me." A warm gust of wind blew her hair over her face.

Strongheart reached out and brushed it away so that he could see her eyes. "White Fawn's father, then, did not say he'd seen you in the forest."

Her face slackened. "Perhaps not then—but sometime I'm sure he told me that."

"You met him?"

"Yes, in Blackbird Town. After Blue Bow was murdered and I was blamed for it, Wink ordered a Healing Circle held for me. As part of the ritual, White Fawn's father came to give me her wedding headdress."

Strongheart gazed out at two mallards that paddled

a short distance away. Their beautiful green crests shone in the fading sunlight.

"Where was Skinner?"

"What?" she asked.

"During the two days he and Flint were apart. Where was War Chief Skinner?"

She ran a hand through her hair. In the past finger of time it had grown damp with perspiration. "I asked Flint about that. I even suggested that Skinner might have killed White Fawn out of jealousy. Skinner loved Flint very much, and he'd lost Flint to a woman once before—to me. Flint told me it was impossible, that Skinner would never have hurt him that way."

"They were lovers?"

"Yes. Flint was blindly devoted to Skinner."

"Were they lovers while the two of you were married?"

She nodded. "Flint told me that every time we argued he ran straight to Skinner for comfort. When he divorced me, Skinner rocked him in his arms for days while Flint wept. For two and half winters, they were happy together. Then Flint met White Fawn . . . and once again things became difficult between them."

The mallards paddled closer, their red eyes on Strongheart and Sora. They murmured to each other, as though discussing the humans sitting on shore.

Strongheart said. "There's one part of the story that has never made sense to me. Supposedly you walked away into the forest before you reached our village, but Chief Blue Bow had warriors everywhere. They surrounded your camp as thickly as the trees." He picked up an acorn that had fallen on the shore and seemed to be examining the shell's intricate colors. "Blue Bow was furious. He ordered two warriors killed over the event."

"Do you think the warriors let me go? Why would they do that?"

He put the acorn back on the shore and pressed it into the sand, planting it. As he covered the nut, he said, "I'm afraid that some of our warriors may have been working with Water Hickory Clan. Certainly our war chief, Grown Bear, was." His gaze lifted to her. "You killed Grown Bear. Do you remember that?"

Her memories were totally blank. "I have no memory of that at all. Are you certain I did it?"

"Not absolutely certain."

"Why would I have killed him?"

"You'd been attacked by the Midnight Fox. After your limbs stopped jerking, I had you taken to my house and placed two guards outside the door. Both of your guards were dead. I found Grown Bear with an ax buried in his head." He piled more sand over the acorn. "Grown Bear was lying on the floor beside several packs of his most precious possessions. He was clearly packed to leave."

"You mean . . . you think he'd planned to escape before the attack came?"

"Yes, which means he knew it was coming. He must have been working very closely with Water Hickory Clan."

As that information soaked in, she wondered how many warriors Grown Bear had bribed to help him. Had Walking Bird led her right into their arms that fateful morning?

She shook her head. "None of this explains my memories of White Fawn."

"No. Not yet." Strongheart gracefully got to his feet and looked down at her. "But it will be dark soon. Do you wish to go back to camp?"

His expression told her that he hoped she would say no.

She looked across the lake. A tendril of smoke hovered over the treetops. Flint had lit the evening fire. Deep inside her, she knew she should go away with Strongheart. He had always believed Flint was a hindrance to her Healing, but . . .

She stood up. "I can't believe he's engaged in secret meetings with his clan."

Strongheart looked at her without blinking, and she had the overwhelming urge to explain, or apologize, but when she started to, he held up a hand to stop her.

"You need to be with him. That's enough for me."

He took the trail that led around the lake and back to their camp.

"SHE'S HERE, HIGH MATRON," CLEARWING SAID. His square face and a patch of his red warshirt were all that showed in the gap in her door curtain.

"Good. Escort her in."

Wink smoothed her hands over her hair. Black and gray strands had come loose from her braid and glued themselves to her cheeks. As she looked down, she noticed that her yellow dress had a thousand wrinkles, but she had no time to change. She rarely met with anyone in her personal chamber; perhaps that alone would be enough to convince Tern this was no ordinary meeting.

She heard the steps coming down the corridor outside and glanced around the chamber, which was ten paces long by twelve wide. The white plastered walls bore magnificent paintings of the gods. To her left, Mother

Sun's golden hair streamed out from her face in flaming spirals. To her right, Comet People streaked earthward with their long blue-white wings tucked behind them. She cast a glance over her shoulder. Right behind her, there was a glorious stylized image of Black Falcon diving into Mother Sun's heart. The dazzling red, purple, and yellow colors looked liquid and shiny. Four sitting mats were arranged around the fire hearth.

"High Matron?" Clearwing said. "Tern, daughter of Elder Bittern, is here, as you requested."

Requested? I ordered her here. She must be seething.

"Please show her in, Clearwing."

Clearwing held aside the door curtain, and Tern entered her personal chamber like one of the Hero Twins preparing to do battle with the monsters of the Beginning Time. She had her pointed chin up and her teeth clenched. Tall and slender, with large dark eyes and a small nose, she had a regal bearing about her—which was good. She was going to need it. Though she had seen only twenty-nine winters, silver already glittered in her short black braid. She'd worn an elegant dress, deep blue, covered with circlets of abalone shell.

Tern stiffly asked, "What do you want?"

Wink did not invite her to sit down. She answered, "It's time that you and I discussed the future of the Black Falcon Nation, Tern. You—"

"Then you should be speaking with Matron Sea Grass, not me."

Hmm. She's bold. In lesser nations, interrupting the high matron could result in the speaker's death.

Wink quietly walked to the bench that lined the wall and picked up the high matron's celt. A ceremonial war club made from red chert, it was long and heavy, stretching from her elbow to her fingertips. The extraordinarily fine flaking gave it a wild crimson shimmer. Reserved only for the elite rulers of the Black Falcon Nation, it was a symbol of the supreme ruler.

With her back to Tern, she said, "Chief Pocket Mouse is in a vulnerable position. Your matron, Sea Grass, has been sending him on more and more war walks. Why do you think that is?"

"My brother is a great leader. He's very valuable to our clan." Her voice was clipped, each word enunciated perfectly.

"Yes, I'm sure he is, but if he were to die in battle, it would leave you in an awkward position." Wink turned to look at her. "Just as my son's death would leave me in an awkward position."

Tern's face showed her confusion. Her delicate brows drew together. "What do you mean?"

Whispers sounded in the corridor—Clearwing speaking with someone.

Tern glanced uneasily at the door.

Carrying her celt, Wink walked to the door, pulled aside the curtain, and called, "Clearwing, please go stand guard at the front entrance."

"Yes, High Matron." He slapped the young warrior he'd been speaking with on the shoulder, and they strode away down the corridor.

Wink waited until their footsteps had faded before

she said, "The actions of your clan elders are endangering our nation, Tern. Surely you are wise enough to see that. You must start thinking about the future. As I am."

Tern seemed to sense the crescendo coming. Her jaw tightened. "Why don't you just tell me why I'm here in your personal chamber, High Matron. This would be a good deal easier if we both knew what we were really discussing."

Wink gave her a small smile. "Yes, I feel the same way."

At last, she gestured to the mats arranged around the fire. "Sit down, Tern. I suspect this will be a lengthy discussion."

Tern hesitated, then walked over and sat on one of the mats with her back rigid.

Wink slowly ambled across the room. As she passed Tern, she extended the ceremonial celt, holding it out for Tern to take.

Surprised, Tern instinctively pulled away.

Wink knelt beside her, picked up Tern's hand, and put the sacred celt in her palm. As she closed Tern's fingers around it, she said, "Perhaps it's time you got used to holding this."

"Matron?" Clearwing's hushed voice woke her.

Wink leaped out of bed and grabbed for her black dress. It had to be just a few hands after nightfall. Breathlessly, she said, "What is it? What's wrong?"

"Matron Sea Grass and three Water Hickory elders are standing at the front door with twenty warriors. They demand to see you this instant."

Wink slipped her dress over her head and ran a comb through her graying black hair. As she hurried for her bedchamber door, she hastily smoothed the wrinkles from her sleeves.

Shouts echoed outside, rising in timbre until they resembled war cries.

Wink ducked into the torchlit corridor and found Clearwing standing outside her bedchamber with his war club gripped in both hands, prepared for the worst.

"Are you afraid they will storm my house?"

"Matron Sea Grass is very agitated. I'm not sure we can predict what she will do."

Wink strode down the corridor for the council chamber with Clearwing right behind her. When she pulled back the curtain to the chamber, she quietly said, "Have someone wake Feather Dancer."

"What about Chief Long Fin and the other elders?"

"No. But after you escort Sea Grass—and only Sea Grass—into the council chamber, I want you to surround this house with one hundred of Rockfish's warriors. Do you understand?"

"Yes, Matron. Right away."

Clearwing marched to the two warriors standing just inside the front door and began issuing quiet but firm orders. Outside, the cacophony of shouts turned into what sounded like a brawl. Clearwing ducked outside, shouted several names, and the scuffling halted.

Wink entered the council chamber and swiftly walked to the fire hearth. A pile of wood rested nearby. She picked up a piece of firewood and placed it on the hot coals. As tiny tongues of flame licked up around the fresh tinder, she added more wood. She was going to need all the light and warmth she could get.

"What are you talking about, you young fool?" Sea Grass said from the corridor. *"These are my personal guards. I go nowhere without them. You will let them accompany me!"*

Clearwing said, "Forgive me, Matron, but my instructions from High Matron Wink are very precise. You—and you alone—are authorized to meet with her tonight."

"That's outrageous! The last Water Hickory Clan matron who met with Wink alone was found mysteriously murdered! I will not be her next victim!"

Apologetically, Clearwing said, "My orders stand, Matron. Either enter alone, or go back to your—"

"Oh, get out of my way!"

Wink heard the old woman's walking stick banging down the corridor. In short order, Sea Grass ducked beneath the curtain with her wrinkled face pinched and her nostrils flaring. "What are you up to, Wink? I was just informed that a large party of Shadow Rock warriors left Blackbird Town just after dark. Where are they going?"

Wink gestured to the four benches that framed the fire hearth. "Sit down and we'll talk about it."

Sea Grass glared, but hobbled forward and slumped onto a bench with her walking stick propped across her lap. Her white hair straggled around her face like frost-killed weeds. Beneath her beaded buckskin cape, she wore only a thin gray dress.

In a hateful voice, Sea Grass said, "I want to know *now!*"

Wink sat on the bench across the fire. For several instants she did not even look at Sea Grass; then, finally she said, "You didn't trust Sora to negotiate for you, did you? You sent your own negotiator, Walking Bird.

How did you get Sora out of the way for those five days?"

Sea Grass' enraged eyes widened in shock for a split instant before she snarled, "I don't know what you're talking about."

"Did you drop a Spirit Plant into Sora's tea? Perhaps her dinner?"

Sea Grass clamped her jaw, but a strange glitter had entered her eyes.

Wink continued, "Walking Bird apparently told Chief Blue Bow that I, personally, had authorized him to negotiate the release of the hostages. Was that your idea? Or your dead predecessor Matron Wood Fern's?"

It never hurt to remind your opponent of the price of treason.

Sea Grass leaned forward. "You're taking grave risks, Wink. My spies will report back on where your warriors go and whom they see. You don't want to do this. Believe me. It will be your doom."

Wink smiled grimly at the death threat. "I'm prepared for that. Are you?"

Sea Grass shouted, "You have no idea what I—!"

Wink rose and walked for the door. Just before she ducked out she called, "Keep your warriors at home, Sea Grass."

She'd made it halfway back to her bedchamber before she heard Feather Dancer's voice and turned to see him striding down the corridor.

He bowed. "Matron. You sent for me."

She watched Sea Grass duck out of the council

chamber, look down the hall to glare at the two of them, then head for the front entry. For a brief instant, Wink looked into the eyes of the other Water Hickory elders: Thrush, Bittern, and Moorhen. They were all old white-haired women with hateful faces. When Sea Grass exited, their questioning voices rose to shouts.

Wink whispered, "Raider made it away safely?"

"Yes. He was surprised that Chief Long Fin was leading the war party, but very honored and grateful. It added to your credibility. Especially since he is your son."

Wink let out a breath and sank back against the wall. The anxiety of the long day seemed to overpower her at once. She yearned to sleep. "Sea Grass can't mount a party quickly enough to catch them, can she?"

"Unlikely. We have a good head start."

She put a hand on Feather Dancer's shoulder, a thing she had never done, and said, "Thank you, War Chief. Now get some sleep. We are both going to need it. This is just the beginning."

SEETHING WITH INDIGNATION, SEA GRASS ROAMED her house swinging her walking stick at anything that didn't move. Shattered pots and overturned baskets lay everywhere, their contents spilled across the floor.

She aimed her walking stick at Chief Pocket Mouse and stabbed him in the shoulder. "If Wink thinks she can bully me, she has a surprise coming!" Sea Grass shouted. "I want you on the trail immediately!"

"Yes, Matron, but . . ." Pocket Mouse had his brown eyes squinted against the emotion in her voice, and it made his flat nose look broader, as though it covered half his face. He'd seen twenty-seven winters, but already lines etched his forehead. "Are we trying to start a civil war?"

"Do you dare to question my orders?" she shouted,

her voice rising to a squeal. "These are the orders of your clan elders, not just mine!"

"I—I did not mean to offend, Matron! Forgive me. How many warriors do you wish me to take?"

"As many as you need to wipe out the entire Shadow Rock war party."

Pocket Mouse mopped his sweaty brow with his red sleeve. "Matron, I'm not sure that's possible. Even if I took all two hundred—"

"I want them dead! I don't care how many warriors it requires, do it!"

Sea Grass hobbled over to glower up into his face. He was a tall, broad-shouldered man. She had to tip her head far back to see his eyes. In a low, threatening voice, she said, "I don't know where her warriors are headed, but it's your job to make sure they do not arrive."

"But, Matron, what about Fan Palm Village? I thought that was our prior—"

"After you've killed the Shadow Rock warriors, destroy it. Just as we planned. Now get out of my sight!" She waved her walking stick to accent her words.

Pocket Mouse deftly dodged the stick, then backed away and hurried from the chamber. As he left her house, she heard him calling orders to his warriors.

Shaking with rage, she hobbled over to her sleeping bench and slumped atop her blankets. "Wink has no idea what I'm capable of. Perhaps it's finally time to order my assassin back to Blackbird Town."

When it grew too dark to see, Sora crawled back into the moldering lodge and slipped between her blankets. She could see Strongheart and Flint talking outside. Flint was angry. Strongheart responded to Flint's every accusation in a calm voice that apparently maddened Flint. Flint finally stamped away, toward Sora's lodge.

When he ducked inside, he said, "Where were you today? I returned to camp to find both of you gone. Strongheart gave me some fool story about going to look for a cave. I was worried about you."

"Were you?"

"Yes, of course I was. I'm the only protection you have against the curs in the Loon Nation." He jerked his shirt off over his head and crawled beneath the blankets with her. "Not only that, I had something important to discuss with you."

"We've been back for over a hand of time, Flint. If it was so important—"

He rolled over, propped himself on one elbow, and whispered, "I don't trust Strongheart."

"Well, we're alone now. What is it?"

Flint peered through the frayed door curtain to make certain Strongheart still stood before the fire finishing his cup of tea; then he dragged her very close. As he looked down at her, their noses almost touched. "I met a Trader today. He told me alarming things."

A Trader. Of course. The man had just been passing by. . . .

But there was something about the way Flint had said it, his tone or the twist of his lips, that made her think he was lying.

Suspicious, she said, "What would a Trader be doing out here?"

"He said he's been forced to beat his way through the brush to avoid the warriors on main trails."

"Warriors?"

He nodded gravely. "Yes, Loon warriors. Apparently the Loon Nation is planning on attacking Blackbird Town."

A surge of fear seared her body. "When?"

"He didn't know. But he said they're massing their forces, calling in warriors from all over Loon country."

Dear gods, can it be true? It makes sense. They must

avenge the murders of their relatives at Eagle Flute Village.

"But why Blackbird Town? It's too big, too well protected. If they were smart they'd start attacking smaller Black Falcon villages, to force us to negotiate."

When the fingers of her left hand started to twitch, she grasped them and held on until they stopped. They'd been spasming like this ever since she and Strongheart returned to camp. It was probably just lack of sleep. Flint had kept an eye on her hands throughout supper.

"I don't think they want to negotiate, Sora. I think they're planning one massive strike at the heart of our nation. If they succeed, they won't have to negotiate. We'll give them whatever they want."

He smoothed his fingers over her face, then down to her throat. As he lowered his head to kiss her, he said, "Don't you find it interesting that you are here?"

Her fingers twitched again, and this time, Flint grasped her hand to hold it still.

"What do you mean?"

"I mean it's very convenient. You are the most valuable hostage they could ever hope to capture. And they got you without a fight."

She pulled away and stared up at him. "I'm not a captive. I wanted to come here."

"You're not a captive *yet*. But I'm sure the Loon leadership knows exactly where you are. You'll be healthy until they need you."

She swallowed hard. The possibility had never

occurred to her, but he was right. The most valuable hostages were kept far away from the fray to make certain they were safe. Then, at the critical moment, when the opposing side needed leverage, the hostage was revealed.

Flint kissed his way down her throat, and she felt his warm mouth on her breast.

"Flint, if I were a captive, surely the Loon Nation would have me under heavy guard. It hardly seems like one priest is enough."

Flint chuckled against her breast. "What makes you think there aren't one hundred warriors watching from a safe distance in the forest?"

She raised her head to look at him. His tongue encircled her nipple before he gently bit it. To think straight she had to fight the sudden warmth that stirred her loins. "Have you seen Loon warriors in the forest?"

"No, but they wouldn't be very good warriors if I had. I'm sure the Loon Nation has their best people out there."

"I don't believe it. I can't be a hostage."

He laughed softly. "Even more tragic is that I am also a hostage. And I'll be the first one they offer the Black Falcon Nation—since I am of lesser value. They'll save you until the end."

Wink despises Flint. She won't bargain for him. She'll let the Loon war chief kill him. . . .

His hand smoothed down her hip and then moved between her legs. She grabbed it to stop him. "Flint, I'm too frightened to enjoy—"

"No, you're not."

He shoved her hand away and tucked his fingers inside her. As he began probing her depths, she arched.

"See," he whispered. "I know you."

Flint rolled on top of her, and a tingling flood rushed through her body. She locked her arms around his back and opened herself to him. Within moments they were lunging against each other as though both of them realized they might not see tomorrow's sunrise.

Just before his seed flooded into her, he lifted his head and gazed down at her with dreamy eyes, saying, "I love you. I have always loved you, Sora. No matter what happens, I want you to remember that."

He thrust wildly.

She gasped at the same time that his cry tore the stillness of the night.

He collapsed on top of her, and for a long time she held him tightly.

When he was on the verge of sleep, she asked, "Flint, where was Skinner during the two days you were apart searching for White Fawn?"

Sleepily, he replied, "I don't know. I wasn't with him. He was out hunting for the wedding procession. Why?"

"Did he travel south toward Eagle Flute Village?"

He yawned. "To do what, Sora?"

"Perhaps to meet someone."

Flint heaved a disgruntled sigh. "Are you still trying to convince yourself that Skinner killed White Fawn? He didn't, Sora. You did."

Pain flickered around her heart. "Yes, I probably did."

"You certainly did." He rolled to his back and slipped his arm beneath his head while he stared sightlessly at the ceiling. In a low pained voice, he said, "I've answered many questions for you over the past quarter moon. Now, I want you to answer one for me. And I want it straight and true."

She lifted herself on one elbow. "What do you want to know?"

His black eyes were like caverns in his handsome face. "Are you in love with Strongheart?"

She hesitated, and he put his hand around her throat and started squeezing. "Are you?"

She grabbed his arm and tried to pull it away, but couldn't. He was so much stronger than she. "I take that as a yes," he snapped, and shoved her away.

Rubbing her throat, she slid to the far side of the lodge and glanced out the door. She did not see Strongheart. He must have retreated to his own lodge farther down the shore.

She said, "You always make me want to run away from you."

Flint aimed a finger at her. "Don't try it. I'll find you. You know I will."

Her skin prickled.

He rolled over, turning his back to her.

How many times had she heard those words? The last winter of their marriage, he'd been insanely jealous. Nearly every evening he'd forced her to get into a canoe with him and row far out into the water, where he'd loved her several times a night. When morning came and she demanded to return to Blackbird Town he'd always hissed in her face, "Don't try to run away from me. I'll find you. You know I will."

She hugged herself to keep from shaking. *Yes, I know you will.*

LIGHTNING CRACKED OVERHEAD AND BRIEFLY strobed the forest. Branches, torn from the towering pines and oaks, tumbled across the ground.

Wink clutched her hood closed beneath her chin and watched the rain-swept darkness for Feather Dancer.

"I think he's coming, Matron," Clearwing said, and stepped in front of her to shield her in case it was not Feather Dancer but a Water Hickory Clan assassin.

His cape whipped around him in snapping folds, blocking much of her view, but she saw the darkness ripple, then glimpsed the two men moving up the trail.

Feather Dancer had one hand twined in Red Raven's cape while the other gripped his war club. His hood had blown back and flapped against his shoulders. Rain drenched his scarred face and plastered his hair to his head.

Red Raven squirmed, trying to break free of Feather Dancer's iron hand. "Let me go!"

Feather Dancer shoved him hard. "Walk."

The ugly little man careened forward with his arms wheeling for balance. "This is ridiculous! Matron Sea Grass has spies everywhere. Within moments she will know where I am!"

"I don't think so. Who would be out on a night like this?"

Feather Dancer used his war club to gesture to Wink. Red Raven squinted, and when he made her out, he said, "High Matron! You should be home before a warm fire! What are you—"

"I'm out here because I thought you might be."

Red Raven stopped a pace from her and glanced uneasily at Clearwing, then Feather Dancer. "What made you think that?"

"My scouts tell me that your trip takes you four days. Two days to get there. Two days to get back."

He grinned sheepishly. "Yes, and the trails to our far northern villages have been badly flooded. I—"

"Which northern villages?" He hesitated too long. Wink said, "*Who* are you meeting with?"

"High Matron"—he extended his hands in a pleading gesture—"the last time you questioned me Sea Grass threatened to have my heart cut out and left bleeding on the floor!"

Lightning flashed again, and his rotted front teeth looked dark and jagged.

Wink drew her cape more tightly about her shoulders.

"That's a much quicker death than the one I'll order if you don't tell me where you've been going and who you've been meeting."

"Please, Matron, I—"

Feather Dancer thumped him hard in the back of the head with his warclub. Red Raven let out a cry and staggered forward. Holding his head, he glared at Feather Dancer. "You'll be sorry," he blurted, "when Sea Grass is the high matron of the Black Falcon Nation! All of you are going to be dead!"

Wink stepped closer to him and stared into his eyes. "Who are you meeting with?"

Red Raven's mouth puckered as though he might cry. He said, "Flint!"

"Where is he?"

His lips pressed into a thin line. "North of Minnow Village."

"What was the last message you carried to him?"

Red Raven shifted his weight to his other foot and looked around. "Matron, I . . ." He must have seen Feather Dancer's club from the corner of his eye, or maybe he heard it whistling through the air, for he yelled and fell to the ground, holding his head. The club sliced the air just above his hands. "High Matron, tell him to stop!"

Wink knelt in front of Red Raven and stared into his eyes. "I don't have much time. I want this over with quickly."

His expression slackened. "What do you mean?"

Slowly, she repeated, "What was the message?"

"Nothing important! Flint is—"

She rose and walked away into the darkness. Behind her, Feather Dancer and Clearwing took turns beating Red Raven with their clubs. Grunts and cries of rage, then pain, filled the darkness.

After thirty heartbeats, the dull thuds of clubs against flesh stopped, and Wink walked back. Red Raven's face was a bloody mess and he had at least one broken rib, for he held his chest and seemed to be having trouble breathing.

She stood over him. "Was it about the attack on Fan Palm Village?"

He shook his head miserably. "No, Sea Grass told him to kill her."

"Who? Kill who?"

Red Raven chuckled hoarsely. "You've been outmaneuvered, High Matron. You're about to lose everyone you care about."

Wink felt like the world had fallen away beneath her feet. *Sora.* Shaky and light-headed, she had to take a deep breath to steady her nerves. "Why?"

"Because Sea Grass doesn't need her any longer."

Wink shook her head in confusion. "What are you talking about?"

Red Raven wiped the blood from his nose and smeared it on his wet cape. "You've been such a fool, High Matron. You still don't know what happened at Eagle Flute Village, do you? You haven't even guessed why Flint took Chieftess Sora there."

"Flint told me . . ." And it occurred to her that at this point anything Flint had told her was probably a lie. "No. Why?"

"Sea Grass ordered him to. The chieftess had killed her son, War Chief Skinner. She figured the Loon People would kill the chieftess; but even if they didn't, they would certainly try her for the murder of Blue Bow, and that would keep them busy while Sea Grass and Wood Fern continued to organize the attack on Eagle Flute Village."

She used the jade to keep me busy and used Sora to keep Eagle Flute Village busy. What an elegant plan. . . .

Red Raven laughed at the expression on Wink's face. "Sea Grass was furious that the chieftess escaped the village massacre. She—"

"Just before she died, Matron Wood Fern told me that Flint didn't know anything about the attack, that he was genuinely trying to Heal Sora."

Red Raven smiled grimly. "Well, that part was true. He didn't know anything about the attack. But as to Healing the Chieftess . . ."

"That's not why he went to Eagle Flute Village?"

Red Raven laughed. "Flint was Matron Wood Fern's best-placed spy. He'd made it into Eagle Flute Village, and they considered him a hero! He could go anywhere, listen to any conversation. Do you think she would have endangered him? Never."

"Then why did Flint—"

"He wanted to avenge Skinner's death more than

any of the rest of us! He's the one who came up with the idea of using the chieftess to get into Eagle Flute Village!"

He tricked me.

Rage warmed her veins, but she lifted her chin and calmly asked, "How did you know Sora was north of Minnow Village?"

He ran his tongue over his rotted front teeth, stalling, before he answered, "In case one of us failed, Sea Grass sent two messengers to tell Flint that if the chieftess had survived the Eagle Flute Village attack, he should take her somewhere and hold her in case we needed her in the future."

"You were one of the messengers. Who was the other?"

"Not even I know that."

The wind had died down. Wink studied the raindrops while she considered her narrowing options. Feather Dancer and Clearwing kept their gazes on Red Raven.

"What message are you carrying from Flint to Sea Grass?"

Red Raven chuckled, but it was an insane sound. "He's trying to convince Sea Grass that the chieftess is still a powerful bargaining tool."

"A bargaining tool?"

"Yes. With you. Flint says you'll do anything to save your friend, including step down as high matron."

He knows me too well—a weakness I cannot afford.

Wink looked at Feather Dancer, nodded, and walked away up the trail. Clearwing was right behind her.

When they were ten paces away, she slowed down and turned to him. "As soon as we return, find Lean Elk. I want to see him right away."

"Yes, Matron."

She'd taken no more than twenty steps when she heard Red Raven's shrill scream rise, only to be cut off in the middle by a dull thunk. A few heartbeats later, another thunk echoed through the wet forest.

She didn't look back.

Feather Dancer caught up with her. "I think we should hasten our plan, Matron. Things are happening faster than we expected."

Wink nodded and took the fork in the trail that led around behind Blackbird Town. She didn't want to walk across the open plaza where anyone would have a clear shot at her.

Just before the mounds came into view, she stopped and looked up at Feather Dancer. In a low voice, she said, "Two of them. Tell our ally. Then we'll talk."

"Tonight?"

"Yes."

Wind ravaged the roof of Elder Moorhen's house, tearing the thatching loose and flapping it against the walls like massive beating wings.

She groggily blinked at the high ceiling. All night long she'd been having trouble sleeping. But it wasn't just the ferocious storm. She kept hearing strange sounds outside her door, snuffling, like a dog in the corridor. Once, she swore she'd heard the scratching of fingers.

"Your shadow-soul probably heard it in your dreams, you idiot."

She rolled to her side and stared at the wall. Sea Grass had been driving them all too hard. The late nights and constant bickering were beginning to nip at her strength. Though Sea Grass kept saying it was for the greater glory of Water Hickory Clan, Moorhen suspected Sea Grass just wanted to rule the Black Falcon Nation.

Not that it mattered. If Sea Grass' twisted plans brought about the fall of Shadow Rock Clan and elevated Water Hickory Clan, it was worth it. Water Hickory was next in line, and Shadow Rock had ruled for centuries. They'd grown stale and weak, too afraid of war to be effective. No nation could afford to have their enemies stop fearing them. Water Hickory Clan would restore that fear and turn it—

Something squealed less than two paces behind her. Her belly prickled. It sounded like wet leather.

A man whispered, "Remain still and there will be no pain."

She started to scream, "Guard—!"

The whir of a war club cut the air.

22

Sora drew the blanket around her shoulders and sank back against the damp wall. Rain fell outside, turning the world utterly dark. The only light came from the smoldering coals in the fire pit two paces away. She deliberately kept her gaze off Flint, who slept on his back with his long hair feathered around him like a black halo, and focused on the glimmering coals. Their crimson color soothed her, making her feel a warmth where there was none.

"You'll never be Healed if he's here," she whispered to herself, barely audible.

A tight band of fear constricted her chest. Through her emotional haze, she caught the scent of damp earth blowing in around the torn door curtain.

"Deep down, you knew this would happen. But you did nothing to stop it."

She closed her eyes and clenched her fists. Her thoughts drifted to Strongheart. The only place she felt safe was close to him. He'd responded to her vulnerabilities in a way she'd never imagined. She'd only wanted him to Heal her. She'd never dreamed . . .

No, don't even think it.

She propped her chin on her drawn-up knees and gazed at the coals; they reddened when the wind fanned them. Never in her life had she felt so broken and vulnerable. How could she mend the damage? The harder she tried to force herself to believe she still loved Flint, the more desperately she longed to escape him. Whereas her love for Flint had always drained her strength, making her feel weak and fragile, her feelings for Strongheart gave her strength. The only time she felt truly alive was when he was looking into her eyes.

She pulled the blanket up around her neck and held it closed. The storm was increasing. Rain pounded the forest, and tiny streams poured through the gaps in the roof of the old lodge. Fortunately, they weren't right over the bedding hides.

She ran her fingers over the soft, finely woven buffalo wool of her blanket.

A shadow moved outside, beneath the sheltering moss-covered limbs of a giant water oak. *Strongheart.*

Sora let her blanket fall and slipped on her dress, then quietly tiptoed to the door and pulled her cape from the peg. As she flipped up her hood and walked out into the storm, wind lashed her cape, billowing it around her.

Strongheart lifted a hand, and she smiled in return.

Despite the darkness, the lake had a faint glow. Standing there, silhouetted against it, Strongheart looked very tall and slender. He had his hood up. Inside, she saw him smile.

"Did I wake you?" he asked as she walked up to stand beside him beneath the mossy canopy, where for the most part it was dry.

"I wasn't sleeping."

"Bad dreams?" he asked, concerned.

"You have to be asleep to dream. My shadow-soul has yet to leave my body."

Out on the lake, geese murmured to each other, and she saw them floating close to shore. They were a paler gray than the lake.

"What's been keeping you awake?" he asked.

She nervously twined her fingers in her cape, and Strongheart noted it with mild interest. The fingers of her right hand twitched. He said nothing.

"I'm beginning to think you were right. We should never have returned to camp."

"Why? Did Flint say something that disturbed you?"

"He told me about the man he saw today. He said it was a Trader."

Strongheart folded his arms beneath his cape. "Really? And what news did the Trader bring?"

She bowed her head. "He told Flint that the Loon Nation is massing warriors for an assault on Blackbird Town."

His brows drew down over his beaked nose. "I certainly hope not. Many more of my relatives will die if my nation is foolish enough to attempt it."

"You don't believe the Trader? You think he was lying?"

Wind tousled his hood, and Strongheart reached up to hold it, to prevent it from blowing back. "Do you really believe Flint met a Trader?"

She suppressed a shiver, and he instinctively lifted an arm, then hesitated to drape it around her shoulders, letting it hover awkwardly. After two or three instants, Sora took a small step forward and eased into his arms. He pulled her close.

"I didn't really intend this," he said. "I was just afraid you were cold."

She hugged him, letting herself drown in the comfort of his arms. "I was."

He pressed his lips to her hair.

She looked up and saw desire in his eyes—before he turned away and forcibly suppressed it.

"Why did you do that?" she asked.

"What if Flint wakes and comes looking for you? What do you think will happen?"

She quickly glanced over her shoulder at the lodge where he slept, then reluctantly pulled away from Strongheart.

They stood awkwardly, barely a hand apart, for a long time before she said, "What made you come out in the storm? Couldn't you sleep either?"

He shook his head. "Power is loose on the wind. The Spirits are restless. They're trying to tell me something, but I'm apparently too dull-witted to understand them."

She glanced around, uneasy. "What Spirits?"

He made a sweeping gesture with his arm. "They're everywhere, Sora. Forbidden Village was only abandoned by the living, not the dead."

"Do you see them?"

"Sometimes. Other times, I hear them whispering to me."

She let her gaze drift over the rainy woods, stopping at every shadow that moved, wondering if it was a Spirit or just a dark bush swaying in the wind.

"You don't see them?" he asked, and gently touched her hand.

"No, and I'm not sure I regret it. Spirits frighten me."

"To tell you the truth, they frighten me, too. But I fear them less than I fear what they might tell me."

Bravely, she tucked her hand into his palm, and he closed his fingers around it. A pleasant warmth flooded her veins. "You mean about the future?"

"Usually it's the future, but on occasion the things they reveal about the past are even more frightening."

"I didn't know Spirits talked about the past." She released his hand and rubbed her arms. Cold bumps had risen on her skin.

His dark hood waffled around his face. "I think they

reveal whatever you need to know to face the future. Often that means telling you about the past."

Anxiously, she asked, "Have they told you anything about my past? Anything that might help to Heal me?"

"About your past? No."

She sensed there was more to it. "Have they told you about someone else's past?"

His dark bulging eyes glinted as he looked down at her, and she had the feeling he was going to tell her something very important . . . but he only smiled and shook his head. "No, Sora. They haven't."

She started to ask another question, but as soon as her mouth opened, Strongheart said, "If Water Hickory Clan ruled the Black Falcon Nation, who would be chief?"

Sora blinked at the suddenness of the question. "Chief? I don't know. Matron Sea Grass would have to choose. With Short Tail dead, it could be Pocket Mouse, I suppose."

"And war chief?"

She narrowed her eyes, wondering why he cared. "If Skinner weren't dead, he would be the first choice. But now? Sea Grass would probably pick someone from Oak Leaf Village, a renowned warrior."

Inside the lodge, Flint said something. It was muffled, as though he was talking in his sleep, but she swung around, panting, as a hot surge of fear raced through her.

Strongheart whispered, "Go back to him. I'll see you

in the morning. I need some time alone to listen to the storm."

He gracefully walked away, heading up the trail that led northward around the lake.

Sora considered following him, but he'd said he needed to be alone. Her belly churning, she turned and walked in the other direction, back to Flint.

"I'M TIRED. LET NO ONE ENTER MY CHAMBER TO-
night," Elder Thrush said to her two guards.

"Yes, Matron."

One of the men yawned, and she scowled at him. It
was very late, but that was no reason for impudence.

They adopted their positions on either side of her
door, and she ducked into her chamber. Instantly, anger
warmed her veins. Her slaves were all lazy! They'd allowed her fire to burn down to coals. There was no excuse for it! She often stayed out very late at meetings.
Tonight should have been no different.

"Mole?" she called. "Sage Cloud?"

Neither slave answered, and it fueled her anger.
Where were they? They knew she didn't see as well as
she used to. If she made it to her sleeping bench by
herself without breaking a hip, it would be a miracle.

She cursed under her breath as she used her toes to feel a path through the darkness. She'd made it halfway across her chamber when a rectangle of torchlight flashed across the floor and retreated. Someone had pulled back her door curtain.

She shouted, "It's about time—!"

Muffled groans sounded in the hallway, followed by two heavy thuds.

Thrush managed to turn in time to see a man she did not know enter her bedchamber.

"What do you want?" she cried. "Who are you?"

He was an ugly man, twice her height, with a pock-marked face. He looked enormous standing in her small bedchamber.

Thrush's head shook. "Did you kill my guards?"

He didn't answer, but she could see a pair of feet thrusting beneath her door curtain and knew it wouldn't do any good to cry for help.

A sick frustration gripped her. She raised her hand and stabbed a finger at him. "Did Wink send you?"

He stepped forward as lightly as a dancer.

"Blessed gods, I can't believe she is this bold!"

The man drew his stiletto from his belt.

Almost in tears, Thrush shouted, "You tell Wink that I *personally* gave the order about her son!"

His bone stiletto flashed in the firelight. . . .

WINK LEANED AGAINST THE WALL JUST OUTSIDE her bedchamber. Her black feathered cape brushed her bare feet. "My son? What did Thrush mean? Did our ally know?"

The dark blue light of predawn streamed around the door curtain at the front of her house and painted the corridor with a faint gleam.

Feather Dancer shook his head. "No. But I wanted to prepare you."

Weary beyond exhaustion, Wink hung her head and said, "Thank you, War Chief. Now get some sleep."

He bowed and walked away. When he ducked out the front entrance, Clearwing entered and hurried to re-sume his position outside her bedchamber.

Wink lifted her door curtain and let it fall silently closed behind her. As she stood staring at the painting of the gods that adorned the walls, a hopeless sensation tormented her.

She clenched her fists and sternly hissed, "Stop it!"

Her souls seemed to be listening. Some of her anxiety seeped away . . . giving her the strength to walk to her clothing basket and begin dressing for what she knew would be a day of shouts and recriminations.

25

As I walk the icy path through the dark-
ness, I feel it; it is a terrified hunger, a need like none I
have ever known. It pulls me as though I am tethered to
it by an invisible rope.

The voice calls again. . . .

It seems to drift in the air around me, and as I
walk toward it, it grows louder until it is almost overpowering.

Strange images flash behind my eyes—darkness that
has never been touched by the light of day, fragments
of memories that do not belong to me, an animal loneliness that I hear in my heart like several packs of
wolves howling in unison . . . harmonic singing.

Somewhere close by fur brushes against stone.

I turn around, searching the darkness for a glimpse,
and see acrid pools of blood drying all around me.

The voice calls again. . . .
Less than a hand's breadth away.
Horror warms my blood.
In front of my face, the darkness becomes a shim-mering midnight blue flood, and in the depths, two enormous eyes blaze to life. . . .

RAIN POURED DOWN THROUGH THE TALL DARK trees and gusted against the old lodges that lined Sassafras Lake, rattling the rotted timbers. A beaten froth scalloped the shore.

Strongheart held his hood closed and took a long drink of his hot tea. Flint stood across the fire from him. He'd been hostile all morning. They'd barely spoken five words since rising, but had gone about their dawn duties, collecting firewood, making the tea, fishing for breakfast. Four catfish, skewered on a long stick, roasted over the low flames. The rich scent filled the air.

"I'm tired of eating fish and birds," Flint announced. Rain sheeted off his cape, creating a dark circle around his feet. "I'm going to go out and hunt deer. I may not be back until after nightfall."

"It's a miserable day to hunt. I was hoping you and I could work together today to Heal the chieftess."

"Do it yourself, Priest."

Strongheart turned the catfish so they wouldn't burn. Already the skins had begun to brown and crisp.

Annoyed, Flint said, "It's strange that Sora hasn't risen. The fish are cooked. Maybe I should wake her."

"No, please let her sleep. She will need it."

Grumbling to himself, Flint reached for a bowl, slid two catfish into it, and began pulling off chunks of flaky white meat. Around a mouthful, he said, "I hate this place." He gestured to the fallen-down lodges of Forbidden Village. "You should have never brought us here."

Strongheart looked around. In the faint half-light, he saw people moving, barely visible even to him, but there nonetheless. Sometimes, he heard curious blends of different accents and languages, and realized they were trying to speak to him, but he could not yet hear them. In time, of course, he would.

In a mild voice, Strongheart said, "You trained him in the use of Spirit Plants, didn't you?"

"Who?"

"War Chief Skinner. You trained him."

Flint tilted his head as though sensing a trap. "Why do you care? It doesn't matter now. None of it does."

"I was trying to figure out how he did it, that's all."

Flint ate another bite of catfish and chewed it while he studied Strongheart. "Did what?"

"You know what I'm talking about."

Flint just stared at him.

Strongheart continued, "The barbarian Lily People were raiding. White Fawn must have been afraid. She would never have allowed a strange woman to get close enough to poison her. But she'd have greeted your best friend with open arms. Skinner could have cooked her dinner himself, and she would have laughed and teased him, without ever realizing what he was up to. Skinner loved you. He couldn't lose you to another woman."

Flint's shoulder muscles contracted and rippled through the fabric of his cape. As he lifted his eyes to Strongheart, scarcely controlled fury laced his voice, "You have no idea how close you are—"

"Did your matron plan to blame Sora for White Fawn's murder? Or was that Skinner's idea, and his alone?"

Flint made a disgusted sound, shoved a huge chunk of catfish into his mouth, and tossed his empty bowl to the muddy ground. "You're a fool, Priest. I'm going hunting. When Sora rises tell her I should be back at dark. But if I'm gone for days, she knows why."

Flint grabbed his bow and quiver from where he'd stashed them beneath the sheltering limbs of a massive cypress tree and slung them over his shoulder. But he stood for several instants staring at his belt from which hung his stiletto and war club. He picked it up and tossed it to Strongheart.

"Guard her," he ordered, and trotted away without another word.

Strongheart tied the belt around his waist and

watched Flint disappear into the downpour, wondering if he was truly going hunting, or had arranged another clandestine meeting with members of his clan.

The scent of charring catfish rose. Strongheart knelt and slid the remaining fish into a bowl, then turned another bowl upside down on top of them to keep them dry and placed the fish on the warm hearthstones.

As he rose to his feet, a coarse guttural sound filtered through the rain.

He looked around.

All of the ghostly apparitions that had been drifting through the forest evaporated, but he could sense them staring at something behind him.

Strongheart turned.

At first, he didn't see . . .

Two glistening eyes peered at him from the depths of Sora's lodge. Dark and unblinking, they had a feral quality, like that of a predator with vulnerable prey in sight.

"Chieftess," he called.

The soft guttural sound blended so perfectly with the falling rain, he wasn't sure he'd heard it.

He walked toward the lodge, and the eyes lowered to the floor, like an animal lying down.

He knelt in the doorway and saw the chieftess stretched out on her stomach with her chin on her folded hands. Long black hair feathered around her naked body.

"Chieftess?" he said again. "Are you hungry? We cooked—"

The faint guttural cry issued from deep in her throat.

Fear crept through his body like an icy night wind. His shadow-soul shouted at him to run, but he girded himself and ducked inside the lodge.

A strange presence moved around him. He could feel the soft nibble of fangs at his throat. Quietly, he asked, "Who are you?"

Something skittered at the base of the lodge, and a bitter loneliness swelled until the ache almost doubled him over. Tears filled his eyes, but he did not know why.

As he removed his wet cape and hung it on the peg by the door, the chieftess licked her full lips. Ordinarily, she was a beautiful woman with large black eyes, delicate brows, and a pointed nose, but this instant she resembled a wary wolf. He . . .

Cold flowed around him, penetrating every gap in his clothing, and he felt like he was lingering on the hazy borderland of death.

Softly, he said, "I've been waiting for you."

She sat up on her haunches and placed her hands on the floor in front of her. "Did you come to give him a home?"

The voice was hers, but deeper, rougher.

Strongheart frowned. He shook his head lightly. "I don't understand."

"Of course you don't understand. How could any sane person believe that he is still alive inside me? He's my heartbeat, my breathing. He's always there looking out through my eyes. It doesn't matter that he's been dead for—"

"Who?" Strongheart asked from a safe distance. The cold had deepened in the lodge. He shivered. "I still don't understand."

"Yes, of course, I know how crazy that sounds. But this madness isn't recent. It started the moment I met Flint. That first moon was one breathless secret rendezvous after another. His best friend, Skinner, or a slave, or a Trader—anyone who wished to help the young lovers—would bring me a message: "He's in the charnel house" or "You'll find him at the canoe landing." Often it was, "Go to him in the forest near the giant redbay tree . . . the dead oak covered with moss . . . the shell midden near the lake. . . ."

"How old were you?"

"I had seen fourteen winters. I loved him desperately. Despite my mother's orders to stay away from Flint, I'd excuse myself from whatever meeting I was attending, and run all the way to meet him. We loved each other in caves and moss-shrouded meadows, even treetops. The massive oak branches provided perfect hideaways where we would lie together for half the day, exploring the other's body, listening to the oblivious people who walked the trails below. The sensations he brought forth during those lazy days of touching left me feeling as though the gods themselves had taught me what it meant to be human. But it was really Flint who taught me. He . . ."

"Taught you? Or taught Sora?"

There was a lengthy pause, as though it did not understand the question. Outside the lodge, something moved, like claws raking the thatch. Strongheart's knees started shaking, though he hoped it wasn't obvious to the Spirits.

"What? I'm sorry, Strongheart, what did you ask?"

He cocked his head, astonished, and asked, "Do you know me?"

No answer. She just stared at him with those black glistening eyes.

He said, "Is that when you awakened? In the first moon they'd known each other?"

The "claws" outside hissed, then scampered around the lodge base. Strongheart spun, trying to keep track of it. Most likely a dead branch had been torn from one of the trees, but . . .

Sora whispered, "No. No, it happened in the first half moon. He talked me into wearing loose-fitting clothing so that no matter where we happened to be, I could just spread my legs and allow him to enter me. Even in the dark moments when his needs shocked me, he managed to make me relax enough that I didn't resist. I remember once, ten days after we met, my mother ordered me to attend a council meeting with her. She was grooming me for my eventual rise to the position of high chieftess of the Black Falcon Nation. Just before the meeting, I met Flint in the forest and he tucked an oiled wooden ball inside me, which he tied in place with a strip of woven hanging-moss cloth expertly passed between my legs and knotted around my waist beneath my dress. Throughout the meeting, whenever I moved, it caressed me. By the time the meeting was over, all he had to do was touch me for waves of joy to explode in my body.

"From that day onward, the carefully selected objects he brought into our life evoked a searing sweetness. It didn't take long before I couldn't even use a stone to pound dirty clothing in the lake without thinking of what Flint might—"

"Didn't his curious needs frighten you?" He did not know if was speaking to Sora or the Midnight Fox, or some strange amalgamation of the two.

"No. Just the opposite. The euphoria intensified over the fourteen winters we were married, probably because our couplings grew progressively more dangerous. He took me wherever and whenever he pleased. During a midnight ceremonial when hundreds of people filled the plaza, he would push me against a dark wall and take me standing up. Or he'd slip a marble owl inside me before I had to discuss a critical Trade agreement; then he would watch my eyes during the negotiations. More than the owl, it was his expectant gaze that brought me pleasure."

Strongheart's hands clenched to fists. The rain battered the lodge and the world seemed to go darker, as though the light were being sucked away into an enormous emptiness. The hair rose on the nape of his neck.

"Don't look at me like that," Sora said. "I'm trying to explain why I had no choice but to kill him."

"You mean you tried to kill Flint. Yes, he told me about that, but I've never really understood why. Couldn't you have just run away from him?"

"No, I couldn't run away! He would have followed

me. He would not leave me alone! And I could not stay away from him. I wanted Flint inside me."

A frantic gleam lit her eyes.

Strongheart held out calming hands. "Please, forgive me. I got lost for a few moments. Let's go back to your first question. You asked me if I'd come to give him a home. Who did you mean?"

Sora's shoulders shook with buried sobs, but no tears filled her eyes.

Cautiously, he reached out and touched her hair. She leaned into his hand, like a lonely puppy. "Can you tell me who he is?"

Her eyes abruptly went wide and searched the lodge. *"Do you see them?"*

"Who? I . . ."

A faint fluttering began at the edges of his vision. Then, all around them, unseen presences moved, stirring the moist air without touching the veils of spiderwebs or skinny arms of dead vines that hung through the gaps in the walls.

He murmured, "Yes, I see them."

"What do they want?"

"I think they are Healers. They want to help you."

Through the pounding rain and whistling wind, Strongheart heard a familiar gravelly old voice, but it spoke just beyond his ability to hear.

"Juggler?"

Lightning flashed outside, briefly illuminating the camp, and an eerie sensation possessed him. The truth seemed to seep out of the very walls, and soak into his body like prickly pear fruit wine—sweet and intoxicating.

He looked back at the Midnight Fox. "Is that it? Do you keep him alive inside you? You've kept him alive all these winters?"

The Midnight Fox heaved a deep relieved breath and closed its eyes. Sora curled up on the buffalohide. Ghostly shadows flitted, moving closer, surrounding Sora in a spectral Healing Circle.

He did not know if he truly heard faint ancient Healing Songs, or if his souls had woven them from the wind and rain, but he sat back on the floor and massaged his forehead. "That's why the murders started. He probably doesn't realize he's chasing away her reflection-soul. . . ."

Sora's body started to quiver, and her eyes rolled back into her head. The seizure struck like a bolt of lightning. She arched and cried out; then her entire body spasmed.

Strongheart leaped to his feet and ran to her. As he dragged her jerking body onto his lap, her teeth gnashed together.

"It's all right." He clutched her tightly against him. "Everything's all right. I understand now."

While the seizure ran its course, he kept whispering, "I understand, Sora. Can you hear me? I understand. . . ."

ROCKFISH GRIMACED. BY THE STANDARDS OF THE Black Falcon Nation, Fan Palm Village was a pathetic conglomeration of sixteen poorly made lodges, crude pottery, and badly woven fabrics. Its only positive attribute was that it sat at the edge of a beautiful meadow, surrounded by hickory and elm trees that shone an unearthly green in the morning sunlight. Corn, sunflowers, and squash fields filled every hollow.

"My village appreciates the gifts sent by your high matron," Chief Sand Conch said, and flicked a hand at one of his wives to take them away.

Perhaps twenty winters old, the woman had a gaunt face and skinny arms. Bars of ribs showed through her dress. She scooped up two of the large baskets and carried them out to the people who had assembled in the plaza. As she began handing them out—first to the elders, then to the others—a cacophony of astonished voices rose. Copper clinked and strings of pearls rattled.

Sand Conch took a long drink of tea, and Rockfish studied him. Skinny and covered with elaborate tattoos, he'd seen perhaps forty winters. To Rockfish, he resembled a brightly colored squirrel. His prominent front teeth thrust outward, giving his face a wedge-shaped appearance. His black hair bun was pinned with an ordinary rabbit-bone skewer. The only jewelry he wore that was of any value was his exquisite pearl necklace.

Rockfish glanced down at Sand Conch's weapons. The Chief's bow and quiver rested at his knee, and he kept his war club across his lap. He was taking no chances.

"High Matron Wink will be pleased that you have accepted her peace offering," Rockfish said, returning to the discussion. "The clan turmoil in the Black Falcon Nation is proving a grueling challenge for our Council of Elders."

Sand Conch's eyes narrowed, "I do not understand why your council doesn't simply Outcast the Water Hickory Clan and be done with it."

"It is a subject of discussion, but no one wishes a civil war."

"Of course not, but Water Hickory Clan is liable to get you entrenched in a long war with other nations, including the Loon Nation. It seems to me that civil war is the lesser challenge."

Rockfish nodded. "High Matron Wink agrees with

you. That's why I'm here, to try to Heal the rift between our peoples."

Sand Conch sighed. "And how does she plan to do that? Many of our relatives are dead."

"First, as partial compensation, she will give you the disputed gathering grounds. Second, she promises a very lucrative Trade alliance." Though as Rockfish looked around, the only thing he could see that the Black Falcon Nation would want was access to their oyster beds.

Sand Conch's brows lowered. "What does she expect in return?"

His wife ran back, grinned, gathered up two more huge baskets, and carted them to the waiting throng of people. As she pulled out rolls of magnificent cloth and pounded copper jewelry, cries of delight and excitement rose. One young woman ripped a pendant from her hand and ran away with a horde of older women chasing her, trying to take it away.

Rockfish said, "High Matron Wink hopes that you will help us to defeat our own rogue clan. Our coordinated efforts will, she believes, end the problem sooner."

"Coordinated efforts. What does that mean? Do you wish us to send warriors to be commanded by your war chiefs?"

The distaste in his voice made it obvious he wasn't about to do that.

Rockfish said, "No. Instead, High Matron Wink will send you warriors to help protect your villages."

Chief Sand Conch lowered his gaze and laughed incredulously. "Forgive me, I do not doubt your words, but given the hostility between our peoples, that seems, perhaps, too generous."

"Too generous to believe, you mean?"

Sand Conch inclined his head in apology. "As I told you, I sent my own emissary to the high matron several days ago. I expect him to return tomorrow morning. If he verifies this exceptional offer"—he made an airy gesture with his hand—"we will talk more. In the meantime . . ."

His gaze shifted when the delighted cries of his people abruptly halted.

Rockfish swiveled to look. The first thing that caught his attention was the dogs. Every cur in the village had stood up and pricked its ears.

"What's wrong?" he asked.

Sand Conch shook his head. "I don't know."

As the molten ball of Mother Sun rose above the treetops, bars of crimson light shot through the highest branches and lanced across the meadow. The sudden quiet seemed unnatural. Rockfish scanned the shadows that streaked the village.

"Look!" a man shouted.

In the distance, across the meadow, three men emerged from the trees, running hard, carrying a litter with a fourth man stretched out on top.

"Hallowed Master of Breath." Sand Conch shoved to his feet, shouting, "War Chief! Rally our warriors!"

A stout burly man in a brown shirt yelled, "Grab your weapons!"

Across the village, men and women ducked into lodges and reemerged carrying bows and quivers, lances, war clubs, and stilettos. They assembled around the war chief, and he immediately dispatched them to guard different parts of the village and forest.

"Who is that?" Rockfish gestured to the litter-bearers. "Can you tell?"

Sand Conch squinted. "The gray-haired man out front is my emissary, Raider. As for the others, their jewelry marks them as Black Falcon warriors."

Rockfish suddenly understood what he meant. As the men ran, their ears, throats, and wrists flashed with copper. They could not be members of the Loon Nation.

"High Matron Wink must have sent them back to guard your emissary."

"I sent my own warriors to do that. Where are they?"

Sand Conch grabbed his bow and quiver and started forward to meet the party. Rockfish had taken two steps when the forest erupted with the hair-raising howls of warriors.

Dozens of people burst from the trees and pounded hard for Fan Palm Village. Over their heads a barrage of arrows arced upward, the fine fletching glinting in the sunlight. As the arrows fell, warriors toppled to the ground, and the screams began. . . .

"Dear gods," Rockfish whispered, "both groups are Black Falcon warriors!"

Sand Conch jerked a quick nod. "It seems your rogue clan is hunting down its own relatives now. Come with me. Let's find out what's—"

Raider broke away from the litter-bearers and sprinted toward Sand Conch, shouting to each person he passed, "Find cover! They'll be here in moments! Run! Run!"

Women grabbed children and scampered for the trees with babies wailing, leaving the village empty except for the warriors crouched behind every lodge and stump, their weapons at the ready.

Raider ran straight to Sand Conch. His dark gray hair was sweat-drenched and matted to his head, and mud filled his wrinkles. "They caught us less than one hand of time ago. We're badly outnumbered."

In a low voice, Sand Conch said, "How many are there?"

"Perhaps two hundred warriors."

Sand Conch's jaw quivered before he clamped it down. "We'll never be able to hold them. We—"

"We might, my chief. High Matron Wink sent you one hundred Shadow Rock Clan warriors to help protect Fan Palm Village. They are the red-shirted warriors out front. With our seventy warriors, we have a chance."

Sand Conch glanced at Rockfish and gave him a stern nod. "It seems you were telling the truth. Then let us fight like brothers."

As Sand Conch lifted his bow, Raider said, "Wait,

my chief. We must find a safe place for Chief Long Fin. He's wounded—"

"Chief Long Fin?" The bottom fell out of Rockfish's stomach. "He's here?"

"Yes, High Matron Wink sent her son to lead our party. He was shot first. I'm sure Water Hickory Clan targeted him deliberately."

"How badly is he wounded?"

Raider shook his head. "I fear he will not survive."

Sand Conch's face paled. He waved to the litter-bearers and ran out toward them, calling, "This way! Bring him this way!"

Rockfish and Raider followed Sand Conch toward the Loon council house, the only structure in the village made of massive upright logs.

As they ran, Raider said, "You are Rockfish?"

"Yes, I—"

"I know who you are. The high matron said you would be her voice in all negotiations with my people. She trusts you. I regret that we meet under these circumstances."

The litter-bearers, panting, followed Sand Conch to the council house and ducked inside.

Rockfish went directly to Long Fin's litter, which rested on the floor near the fire hearth. The young chief's arms flailed at nothing.

"Long Fin? It's Rockfish," he said as he knelt down and examined Long Fin's blood-soaked cape.

"Rockfish . . . ," Long Fin murmured. He couldn't keep his eyes still.

He can't see me.

Rockfish ripped open the cape and saw the arrow still buried in his right side. It had been snapped off near the skin, probably when Long Fin fell after the shot, which meant getting hold of it to pull it out would be very difficult.

"Long Fin, you've lost a lot of blood. I'm going to bandage your wound. Try not to move." He reached down and ripped off the bottom of his tan knee-length shirt.

"Rockfish, tell Mother . . . tell her . . . I'm sorry." His eyes swam around in his skull.

"You have nothing to be sorry for. This isn't your fault."

"No, tell her I'm sorry . . . for being . . . a bad chief. I'm sorry."

"You are a good chief, Long Fin. She told me so herself."

It wasn't true, but it didn't matter.

A faint smile came to Long Fin's face.

The sounds of battle loomed closer. An arrow smacked the council house, followed by several more.

"Come with me!" Sand Conch slapped Raider on the shoulder. "Tell me which Black Falcon warriors I can kill, and which I can't!"

28

"OH, STOP CACKLING LIKE A SCARED GROUSE!" SEA
Grass ordered.

Elder Bittern folded her wrinkled hands in her lap
and quavered, "We should never have sent all our
warriors after the Black Falcon party! It's taken Wink
less than two days to kill the few warriors we ordered
to stay here to guard us. What were we thinking?
We—"

"We were thinking we wanted them all dead, that's
what!" She waved her walking stick, and the torchlight
cast her shadow on the walls like a battling giant.

Bittern smoothed a loose strand of white hair away
from her withered mouth and whispered, "I'm next. I
know I am. Wink is saving you for last. I just can't figure out why she hasn't killed both of us already."

Sea Grass gripped the head of her walking stick with both hands and snapped, "Stop thinking about yourself."

"Well, what else do I have to think of?"

Sea Grass glowered. "Ten winters from now."

"I won't see the next ten winters, Sea Grass! Neither will you!"

Sea Grass smiled sourly. "No, but your son, Chief Pocket Mouse, will—unless he's killed in battle, of course."

Bittern wiped her eyes. "What do you mean?"

"I mean that by now Fan Palm Village is a pile of ashes. Chief Long Fin is dead, and our warriors are hunting down the last of the Shadow Rock war party. In the end, we will still win. Water Hickory Clan will rule the Black Falcon Nation. Pocket Mouse *will* be chief."

Bittern's eyes widened.

Sea Grass smiled grimly. "Yes, think about it. Sora cannot have children, and Long Fin was Wink's only child. When they are gone, the leadership will naturally fall to our clan."

"Then my daughter . . ." Her voice trailed away in awe.

Sea Grass nodded. "Yes, Tern will be high matron. There's nothing Wink can do to stop it now."

Bittern's smile faded. "Unless, of course, the other members of the council vote to Outcast our clan."

Sea Grass shook her head. "Improbable. Once we're dead, the other matrons will believe justice has been done. They'll find it too distasteful to punish the innocent members of Water Hickory Clan. Trust me, I know my rivals."

The door curtain whispered behind her.

Wink stepped into the chamber, alone. Her crimson dress was regal; freshwater pearls covered the entire top half. But she looked pale and lifeless.

Sea Grass' mouth twisted distastefully. "Where's your assassin, Lean Elk? I expected to see him last night."

"Off on another mission."

Bittern started crying softly.

"Stop it or I'll beat you with my walking stick!" Sea Grass ordered.

Bittern buried her face in the hem of her cape, which somewhat muffled her cries.

Wink clenched her fists at her sides. She seemed to be studying Sea Grass' every wrinkle and age spot.

"Well, what is it?" Sea Grass said. "Did you come to gloat or to bargain?"

Softly, Wink replied, "I just wanted to see your face one last time."

She turned and walked out of the chamber.

The curtain whispered behind her.

"Stand a few paces away, Clearwing. This will be a private discussion."

"Yes, Matron."

Wink ducked out through the rear entrance of the Matron's House and found Birch waiting for her on the log bench that rested against the wall. Birch had her white hair pinned in a bun on top of her head. Her dress blew around her sticklike arms.

Wink sat beside her, and Clearwing walked four paces away. He stood with his bow down, but nocked, his eyes scanning the foreground.

"Just tell me if this is your doing?" Birch asked.

"I'd rather not."

Birch turned to peer at her with her mouth tight. "I feel the same way you do, Wink, but this sets a dangerous precedent. If you can kill the elders of another clan for political gain, they can kill your elders."

Wink exhaled hard, nodded.

Birch turned away to gaze out at the flowering dogwood trees on the cliff behind Blackbird Town. Their sweet scent carried on the wind. "The rest of the council knows nothing about this, is that it? You are purely to blame?"

Wink stared down at her hands. Her nails were torn and dirty, the cuticles bitten to the quick. "When this is all over, Birch, whoever remains on the council will be forced to make a decision about Water Hickory Clan. I still believe civil war is the worst outcome. We must remain united, or the Black Falcon Nation will collapse. Do you understand what I'm saying?"

A lock of white hair blew loose from Birch's bun and fluttered in the breeze. "You are setting yourself up to be the sacrificial offering."

"The Law of Retribution will demand that both sides pay."

"Ah, I see," Birch said softly.

Wink breathed in the fragrant air and closed her eyes for a few blessed moments. She was so tired she couldn't keep her head from wobbling.

Birch said, "Well, you certainly have them on the run. I guess you scared them silly this morning. Bittern and Sea Grass have been hiding in the Water Hickory Matron's House all day long. Sea Grass has two guards left, out of twenty."

Not for long. . . .

Wink studied the golden gleam that swirled behind her closed lids. If she let herself, she could fall asleep right now, in a single heartbeat, and Birch might not notice for twenty. The possibility was tempting.

Birch leaned closer to her to whisper, "Rumor has it that at nightfall, Sea Grass is going to try to sneak out of town and make a run for it."

"She may make it."

Birch shifted on the bench. "Really? Why?"

Wink opened her eyes and through a long exhalation said, "Because I haven't decided about her yet."

"Why not? She's the worst of the lot."

"I know, but there has to be a witness. Someone to pass along the story."

Birch made a flip-flop gesture with her hand. "Well, she's not the one I'd choose, but since I know nothing about this—"

"Who would you choose?"

"If it were up to me, I'd select Bittern's daughter, Tern."

Wink opened her eyes, but she saw nothing outside. Her souls were traveling down the long road that led into the future. "I can't do that."

Birch's brow furrowed. "She's the best choice. Do you know why?"

"Of course I know why. Don't be insulting."

Birch chuckled. For a while, they just sat together in companionable silence, and Wink was deeply thankful that Birch had asked for this meeting.

Wink rose to her feet. "You are my friend, Birch. I will never forget that."

Birch got up and smiled. "Never plot alone. It takes too much strength. Besides, plotting happens to be the one thing I'm good for these days. Otherwise I just sit in my house listening to one person after another tell me about their squabbles with their neigh—"

"*Matron*?" Clearwing called.

"Yes?"

"Feather Dancer just trotted out into the plaza to meet a runner. The poor man looks half-dead. He stumbled into town and collapsed in a heap. A crowd has gathered around them."

Wink frowned and walked over to stand by Clearwing, where she could see the plaza. Feather Dancer crouched beside the man, who was coughing and weeping while he told his story.

"Who is that? Can you tell?"

"No, Matron. Not from up here."

"Perhaps I should go down—"

"Please don't. If it's important, Feather Dancer will be here shortly."

Wink nodded, and Birch came up beside her. Something was wrong; Wink could feel it like an earthquake deep inside her, getting stronger, set to tear her world asunder.

Feather Dancer rose and ran hard for the Matron's Mound.

Birch said, "Well, there's your answer. It's very important. Do you want me to leave, or stay?"

"Stay. If you don't mind."

"I don't."

Feather Dancer raced around to the rear of the Matron's House, bowed halfheartedly, and said, "Matron, I have news of the Fan Palm Village battle."

"What happened?"

"The Water Hickory warriors caught ours just before they made it to Fan Palm Village. There was a skirmish in the forest. Our warriors were greatly outnumbered. They fought a valiant retreat into Fan Palm Village." Feather Dancer paused to take a breath.

"Hurry, War Chief, finish the tale," Wink said, not able to stand it any longer.

"Every warrior in Fan Palm Village joined ours. They fought side by side to drive back the Water Hickory assault. The tide changed many times during the day, but by nightfall, our forces had decimated the Water Hickory warriors. The few survivors fled for their lives."

Clearwing grinned broadly until Feather Dancer gave him a stern look.

Birch sighed. "Well, at least that's good news. Did the Loon warriors fight valiantly, or were they mostly cowards?"

"I heard that they fought very bravely, Matron," Feather Dancer said.

"Hmm," Birch grunted as though amazed. "They may make worthy allies after all."

Wink braced her shoulder against the log wall. Her

knees were shaking. She didn't know how much longer she could keep standing. "Any word from Rockfish?"

"Yes, but I'd rather tell you in private."

She straightened. The knot of suspicion around her heart had begun to tighten until it was almost a certainty. It took effort to force herself to say, "Tell me quickly."

Feather Dancer was blunt. "The Water Hickory warriors apparently had orders to target Chief Long Fin first. He's dead."

The blood drained from her face as a thousand images flitted across her souls at once: his birth . . . his smiling little boy face . . . the tears of his first broken heart. . . .

Birch grabbed her arm and whispered, "Let me take you to your bedchamber where you can lie down."

Wink didn't answer. She stared at Feather Dancer. "How did he die?"

"The arrow pierced his liver. He bled to death. Rockfish was with him."

An unearthly sense of gratitude filled her. She whispered, "At least he wasn't alone."

Birch said, "Come along. Let's go inside."

Wink just stood for a few moments with her eyes closed, trying not to see . . . anything. A black cavern was forming in her chest. At the end of her days, when she stood before her ancestors in the Land of the Dead, she would be called upon to account for this. Dear gods, how would she do it?

She said, "Thank you, Birch, but I still have many things to do today. It would help me if you could tell Tern that I wish to see her."

Birch released her arm. "Yes, of course."

Wink ducked through the rear entrance and numbly walked to her bedchamber. Clearwing took up his position outside.

She made it almost to the sitting mat by the fire hearth before she stumbled, sank to the floor, and her shoulders began to heave.

After too long a time, she forced herself to get up. To prepare for Tern's arrival.

STAR PEOPLE GLITTERED THROUGH THE THIN layer of clouds, turning the trees and old lodges silver.

Strongheart draped a blanket around Sora's shoulders and handed her a cup of tea to go along with her bowl of catfish. She set the cup aside, pulled off the crisp fish skin, and ate it while her eyes probed the dark forest. Though she had been awake for nearly one hand of time, she could not shake the deep-seated fear that twisted her belly. "How long was I gone?"

"Two days."

She stared into his eyes. A knowledge lived there, something old and deep, as though after a lifetime of searching he had finally deciphered the nature of the gods.

"I'm sorry," she said in an exhausted voice.

"There's no reason to apologize. You can't control

your illness." He knelt to her right and retrieved his own cup of tea. As he drank, the firelight cast an amber gleam over his round flat face. "Besides, we had a good long talk, about Flint, among other things."

She ate a chunk of fish and swallowed it as she looked around. "I don't remember any of it."

"Doesn't matter," he said, "I do. I—"

"Where is Flint?" she asked, suddenly panicked.

Dear gods, he must have gone out into the forest and the warriors captured him. He may be dead. . . .

"He went hunting. He said he'd be back by nightfall. I'm sure he'll return soon."

Don't think about it! There's nothing you can do now. You're a captive. You have to figure out how to escape. . . .

The feel of Flint's hands around her throat two nights ago suddenly intruded, but her memories played tricks on her, transposing Skinner's hands for Flint's, and then Flint's for Skinner's. On the terrible night Skinner died, he'd tried to choke her to death.

"Sora?" Strongheart whispered, as though not wishing to disturb her thoughts. "Did you hear me?"

"Forgive me, I didn't hear you. I was lost in memories of things that happened over a moon ago. What did you ask?"

"I asked about the Midnight Fox. You had seen six winters when the Midnight Fox first appeared to you, is that right?"

"No, I had seen seven winters." He knew that. Why had he deliberately gotten it wrong?

"You discovered him just before your father's death. Why? What made you notice him?"

She cocked her head, wondering what he was doing. "I discovered him a few days *after* my father's death. You see, he glittered. When I looked more closely, I noticed that he resembled an animal lying curled on a dark forest floor. A midnight-colored fox, I thought. I could just make out his shape, but I was entranced by his sheer size. How could an animal that big live behind my eyes? In time I learned that he was not merely darkness. He was a darkness that saw. That spoke. And he was just a baby. He would grow. As I would."

There! There's a warrior out in the trees! I see him moving from trunk to trunk. . . .

When tears filled her eyes, Strongheart reached out to her.

"No, don't touch me, Priest," she said, and wiped her eyes, all the while trying to see through the smoke-colored trees to the warrior prowling the darkness. "I'm all right. I just can't help shaking when I remember."

"Flint tried to Heal you, didn't he?"

"Yes, of course, Flint tried. He thought he could kill the Fox. Then one night he woke to find the Fox staring down at him from my eyes. I was very happy. I knew that he must finally understand."

In a voice almost too soft to hear, Strongheart asked, "What did you think he would understand?"

"But it's perfectly clear. How can *you* not understand?"

"Sora, most humans see themselves as the tormented, rarely as the tormentors. Rarer still is the person who glimpses the murderer within. That's why killing is a kind of desperate mourning." He tipped up her chin to look into her eyes. "Do you agree?"

She massaged her temples. "Yes, I agree that killing is a kind of mourning, but I killed no one. If murder was done, it was done by the Fox."

No one believes me. No one ever has. But it doesn't matter now. Eventually, the warriors will come for me and the Loon Nation will order my death. . . . I must prepare myself.

A gust of wind assaulted the forest and flipped off the blanket that covered her shoulders. Strongheart rose and draped it over her again. "I want you to think about my next question before you answer."

She lifted her head to peer at him, and he said, "Who are you mourning?"

"Who am I mourning? I'm not mourning, I . . ."

The words died in her throat.

She sat back on the buffalohide and stared up at the Star People who spread across the night sky like a great dark blanket covered with sunlit seashells.

"I mourn them all. My father, my sister, my mother. Others. What does that have to do—"

"Everything, Sora," he said in the kindest voice she'd ever heard. "In fact, it's the heart of the matter."

He waited, sipping his tea, as though he could not give her the answers. She had to find them for herself.

But all I can think about is how close the warriors

are. They must move in at night, tightening the circle, lest I try to escape under the cover of darkness.

She shivered. "I don't understand why Flint isn't back yet. He said he'd return at nightfall?"

The lines around Strongheart's mouth deepened. "He said something else."

"What?"

"He said, 'If I'm gone for days, she knows why.' "

She reached for more catfish, and her hand shook. She tried not to notice how Strongheart's gaze remained on her, silently asking questions she did not want to answer. After she swallowed her fish, she said, "We argued."

Strongheart pointed to his own throat. "Is that where the bruises on your throat came from?"

She reached up to touch them. "I didn't know they were there."

"They are."

As though angry with himself for letting Flint hurt her, he clenched his jaw and looked out at the starlit lake where geese floated soundlessly, their bills tucked beneath their wings. Occasionally they quacked to each other in soft intimate voices. "What did you argue about?"

"He told me about the warriors."

Strongheart frowned as though he had no idea what she was talking about. "What warriors?"

"The—the warriors. Hiding in the trees." She pointed out at the forest and started trembling again.

"Sora, there are no warriors in the trees."

She shook her head fiercely. "It—it's all right. I understand. In the same situation, I suppose I'd have you guarded as well."

He blinked and set his tea cup down. "How many warriors did Flint say there were?"

"A-at least one hundred."

Strongheart's mouth quirked. Then he laughed out loud. "Really? I wonder why he felt free to go hunting? You'd think a hundred warriors would have made him nervous—even two warriors would have given me pause."

She cocked her head in disbelief. "Why do you think it's funny? I don't like being a hostage, Strongheart. I wish you'd told me."

In less than a heartbeat, his smile faded to a dire expression. "Sora, there are no warriors out there. None. You are not a hostage."

"Y-yes," she insisted. "There are warriors. I—I've s-seen them." To stop the stutter she clenched her fists and shook them. "It's all right. I understand!"

Thoughts churned behind his eyes, but he sat perfectly still. Then something changed; it was as though his eyes began glowing from an inner light. "Dear gods," he whispered, "that's how they did it."

"What?"

"Sora," he said her name with such warmth it left her floundering. "Please tell me something. Just before the Midnight Fox attacks you, is there anything that happens? Anything that lets you know he might be waking?"

She lifted her hands and held them out, palms up to the firelight, which flowed across the surface, shadowing the lines. The tracery resembled the complicated web of a poisonous spider. Stunned by the sudden realization, she said, "My fingers twitch."

"They twitched two nights ago. I saw them. Do you recall?"

"No, I—I don't."

"Flint must have seen that happen many times over the fourteen winters you were married."

She lifted a shoulder. "Maybe. I can't say for certain."

As though talking to himself, he whispered, "The story about Walking Bird. Flint knew exactly how to plant it."

She leaned over and put a hand on his. "Knew what?"

He gritted his teeth, clearly upset with himself for not having concluded this before. "I may be wrong, Sora. They could just as easily have staged it after giving you a Spirit Plant."

She repeated, "Knew what, Strongheart?"

He turned to her. "Let's talk about Flint, shall we? Would you say he's a sensitive man, and proud of it?"

"Yes."

"I suspect he sulked over every unkind word as though it were a tragedy of monumental proportions?"

She nodded in surprise. "Yes, I used to be terrified of saying the wrong thing because he acted as if I'd tried to cut out his heart. He'd punish me for moons."

"His mother must have lived in terror of hurting his wonderful delicate feelings."

His words carried no hint of reproach; he was simply stating what must have been the case, but it was as though he was fitting together the broken pieces of a pot, seeing for the first time what it might have looked like, and finding the shape ugly.

Sora replied, "She did live in terror. She once told me he threw the worst temper—"

"Sora"—he touched her cheek—"Flint uses his hurt feelings to tyrannize those who care about him. He loves playing games. He has a vulgar infantile streak. A dangerous one."

"What does that mean? I thought all men were like that."

Strongheart's serious expression dissolved to a smile. He obviously couldn't help it. "No, at least I certainly hope not." He shook his head as though to shake off the mirth, and continued. "Men like Flint are weak. They so fear that their vulnerabilities will be discovered that they must find everyone else's vulnerabilities first. They use them like weapons." He hesitated, and his eyes narrowed again. "He knows your vulnerabilities very well, doesn't he?"

"Yes."

"I believe he may be using them for the benefit of his clan."

The words struck at her heart. Despite all the horrors they had inflicted upon each other, she'd never stopped loving Flint. Stubbornly, she insisted, "There are warriors in the trees, Strongheart. I know there are. I've seen them!"

"I know you *think* you've seen them. I don't doubt that, Sora. But they aren't there. Flint wants you to think you need his protection."

Anxiety stitched her chest. Her gaze darted over the dark trees and out across the starlit lake. She wanted to believe him, but . . .

I did see them . . . didn't I?

Sternly, she said, "Look me straight in the eyes and tell me I am not a hostage."

He leaned toward her and said, "You are not a hostage. There are no warriors."

She searched the depths of his eyes for some hint of deception, but found none. "But . . . I would swear to you that I saw warriors skulking through the trees."

Deep inside her, her souls looked at the images again—dark shadows leaping between trunks . . . running through the brush . . . climbing high into the treetops. . . .

"Chieftess, what I'm about to say may sound like babbling, but please listen."

"Of course."

"I have treated many cases of the Rainbow Black. Just before the sick person collapses, she is very susceptible to storytelling."

"What does that mean?"

"I don't know how to explain it, but I suspect the reflection-soul flees the body at the first sign of the attack. When it returns the only way it can explain the things the body heard while it was gone is that they must be true memories."

Confused, she squinted at him. "You mean the memories aren't real."

"The memories *are* real, but they're memories of a story, not a real event."

A sudden loneliness clutched at her belly. She gazed up at the glittering Star People and felt that she, too, had lived in utter darkness her entire life. She'd never really understood the important things. Somehow she seemed incapable of looking straight into the eyes of her souls.

Strongheart must have read her expression. He took her hand. "I have a gift for you. And a task."

"A gift?"

"Yes. Please, follow me." The deep calm of his voice mesmerized her.

Fatigue weighted her shoulders like a granite blanket, but she forced herself to stand, and to follow in his footsteps along the sandy shore. A finger of time later, she saw a freshly built domelike lodge; it sat on the very edge of the lake, two paces from the water.

"You built a new lodge? I'm so glad," she said, her spirits lifting. "I was getting very tired of the smell of moldering wood."

She started to walk to it, but he grasped her hand. They stood eye to eye for several moments. His gaze caressed the starlit glints in her hair, the smooth lines of her face. She could feel her pulse increasing.

He said, "There's something else I must tell you. About the task, but not just yet."

"Why not? What is it?"

He released her hand and gently wrapped his arms around her. A surge of warmth flooded her veins. It felt soothing to be held by him. She pulled him against her, holding him tightly, and he bent and kissed her. His lips were soft and enticing, and she melted against him, her body conforming to the hollows of his. In the back of her mind, a voice whispered, *I'll find you. You know I will. . . .*

"Strongheart, I—I—"

He held her tightly, whispering in her ear, "Don't listen to his voice, Sora. Just be with me."

"But he said—"

"It doesn't matter."

She stood rigid in his embrace, shaking. "He asked me if I loved you."

Strongheart's hold slackened, and he looked down. "What did you say?"

"Nothing. I didn't want him to know."

For a long time, their gazes held; then he took her hand and led her into the lodge.

Three body lengths across, and two tall, it smelled sweetly of fresh-cut pine saplings and thatch made of spring grasses. A buffalohide rested in the rear; the dark brown hair glimmered in the crimson light cast by the fire's coals.

In a graceful motion, he untied Flint's weapons belt

and dropped it by the door. "Tonight is the night, Sora. I can't wait any longer." He gestured to a white-and-black painted pot that rested on the hearth stones. "The task will be difficult."

She took a deep breath, preparing herself, and noticed that a faint bitter odor permeated the air. At first, she thought it was pine resin, then . . .

"The doorway?" she asked.

He nodded. "The ritual is much easier when there are two people, but Flint is clearly not interested in helping me. The two of us must do it alone."

She hated the very thought of drinking a Spirit Plant tea, but she heaved a sigh and said, "What must I do?"

"COME AND SIT WITH ME ON THE BUFFALOHIDE,"
Strongheart said.

Sora let him lead her to the rear of the house, where
he gestured for her to sit down.

For a time, he didn't speak. He went to the hearth,
pulled branches from the woodpile, and added them to
the coals until the flames leapt and crackled. When he
rose, he picked up the small pot. The flames threw his
tall shadow over the walls. The expression on his face
was calm and knowing.

He came back and sat beside her. As he extended the
pot, he said, "Drink it slowly."

She took the pot and sipped the tea. A bitter moldy
flavor coated her mouth. She took another sip. "Is it
the skunk cabbage or the thorn apple seeds that give it
this awful flavor?"

"Both." His lips turned in a faint smile. "Please remember that if the gods decide to help us, the door will open."

"How will I recognize it?"

"It is a dark hole in the world. You'll know immediately what it is."

She took another sip and winced. "Where does the doorway lead?"

"Into the forests of the Land of the Dead."

A shudder ran up her spine. In a frightened whisper, she asked, "Why am I going there?"

"There's someone you must see."

Firelight reflected in his dark eyes.

She stared at him. "Who?"

He gestured to the cup, and she realized she'd stopped drinking. *My souls don't want to do this any more than I do.*

She lifted the tea and took a long drink, then another. A curious sensation seeped through her blood. . . . She felt as though she were floating on a calm vast ocean. She finished the tea and handed him the cup.

Strongheart took it and set it aside. "Are you ready?"

"No, but tell me what to do."

Strongheart pulled his shirt over his head. His magnificent tattoos gleamed. Her gaze clung to the bands of interconnected human eyes, red and black, that ringed his muscular legs from groin to ankles. They seemed to blink in the firelight. His short black hair framed his round face, making his large sad eyes seem to bulge even more. A fine mist of perspiration covered the arch of his hooked nose.

She let him pull away the blanket that draped her shoulders; then he slipped her dress over her head and placed it to the side. Despite the flames, the cool night wind that breathed through the doorway ate into her skin. She rubbed her arms to keep warm.

Strongheart gestured to the hide. "Lie down beside me."

Sora stretched out facing him and looked at his lean, muscular body. Her souls felt awash, rocking like a tiny boat in a sea of warmth.

"Stay here with me," he said, and lightly placed a hand on her arm. "Try not to let your shadow-soul walk the same paths it has with Flint. It must head directly to the Land of the Dead."

"I'll try."

"Good." He brushed his lips against her throat. They felt cool and soft.

She shivered, and he reached down and pulled the blanket up over them, asking, "Better?"

"Yes."

Strongheart smoothed his hand down her arm to the tips of her fingers. His touch was so light, she almost didn't feel it. For one hundred heartbeats, he trailed just his fingertips over her skin, never lingering anywhere for long, circling her nipples, following out the lines of her ribs, then her hip bones, drawing downward as though outlining her right leg bones, toes, moving to her left leg, and rising. When his fingers moved between her legs, she shuddered, but his fingertips only lightly glided over her opening and little manhood before they proceeded up her belly.

"Are you all right?" he asked. "Are you still here, with me?"

"I'm here," she answered.

He lifted his hands to warm them before the flames; then he placed his fingertips on her forehead and smoothed them around her hairline. The tension in her shoulders eased. He lightly traced the bones of her cheeks, and brought his fingers down around her jaw to the point of her chin. Then his hands dropped to her breasts, and he caressed them with exquisite patience.

She had a quick glimpse of Flint's jealous eyes, and she—

"Where is your shadow-soul walking, Sora?"

"I'm sorry. Paths I've walked with Flint."

"Come back to me. Concentrate on me."

She concentrated on the feel of his hands, the warmth they stirred in her body. No man had ever touched her this way, with this infinite tenderness. It frightened her a little.

"You're trembling," Strongheart whispered. "Are you all right?"

"I'm afraid."

"Of me?"

"No. I—in my entire life, I've never wanted any man but Flint, but now—"

At the mention of Flint's name, Strongheart kissed her. His lips were like warm velvet. A tingle ran through her body, and a shimmering halo of light swelled around him. She marveled at how it glittered in his hair and flowed like liquid sunshine over his skin.

Against her mouth, he whispered, "Do you see me?"

"Yes, you—you're glowing." Tears filled her eyes. She did not know why, but they trailed down her face.

He patiently wiped them away, then took her in his arms and laid his cheek against hers. The tension of a thousand winters seemed to drain away. She slipped her arms around his back and pulled him down on top of her, clutching his tall body like a shield against her memories.

Into her ear, he said, "The glow is going to grow brighter and brighter. Stay here with me for as long as you can, then let yourself walk down the path of light, and it will lead you to the underworld. But I need you to tell me when Flint comes into your heart."

"So you can defend yourself?"

"Yes. And you."

He pressed his lips to her hair, and a branch broke in the fire, filling the lodge with sparks that whirled upward toward the smokehole. They joined the brilliant halo around his body and began a dancing, spiraling conflagration.

As she watched them, she murmured, "I love you."

He didn't move. He kept his lips pressed to her hair, and she could feel his soft, steady breathing. After a moment, he replied, "Yes, I know you do."

The sparks spun like tiny tornadoes before being sucked up through the smokehole and out into the night. Because he had not told her he loved her, she didn't feel pity for him. Had he done that to keep her from walking down the "same paths" she had walked with Flint? It made—

"Stay with me, Sora."

She squeezed her eyes closed, blocking all memories, focusing only on the blinding light and the sensations he stirred in her body.

He tenderly touched the inside of her thigh, and she opened herself to him. To her surprise, he did not enter her. He lay with his body pressed against hers, his chest rising and falling in a steady, comforting rhythm. No matter how hard she tried to fight them, images of loving Flint appeared and disappeared on the fabric of her souls.

Strongheart pressed his cheek against hers. "Do you have a favorite memory of being with me?"

She thought about it. "Yes. The first night in Eagle Flute Village. After Flint had dragged me into the forest to rape me, you came to get me. You—"

"Close your eyes and think about that. Try to remember every detail."

She took a deep breath and let her soul drift backward in time.

It seemed to take forever before she found the right moment. . . .

I shakily walk back to the village with my heart an open wound. Behind me Flint and the two Loon warriors, Snail and Black Turtle, laugh. He has promised them that if they help him, he will let each have a turn with me. I clench my hands to fists to keep my mind off the fact that I long to lie down in the grass and weep.

Through the trees, I see Eagle Flute Village: crude thatched houses, hungry people, things I have feared my entire life.

As I step out of the forest, soft murmurs fill the air. Every eye is upon me. I draw myself up and march straight to the guards standing in front of the Captives' House, where I am being held, and order, "Get out of my way."

The big man tips his chin to something behind me, says, "I have orders to hold you for him."

Strongheart flows through the darkness as though part of it. His cape billows around his long legs. When he gets closer, he glances at Flint and says, "I'm sure you won't object if I, too, take a turn with her."

My heart goes cold and dead in my chest.

Flint . . .

Strongheart whispers, "Don't think about him, Sora."

She swallowed hard and nodded.

As we walk, Strongheart says, "You're shaking. Did they hurt you?"

"*No. Given more time, they might have, but Flint was in a hurry.*"

He leads me to his house and holds the door curtain aside. "*Go in. There are warm blankets by the fire. You must be cold.*"

I duck into his house and look around. The firelight silhouettes the baskets and pots that sit beneath the bench encircling the walls. Blankets rest beside the fire, as though prepared for me. I walk to them and ease down.

Strongheart kneels to my right and studies me for a long time. He gestures to my bleeding mouth. "*Which one did that?*"

"*Flint.*" *I touch my lip and wince.* "*He was a little too 'eager.'*"

Strongheart doesn't say a word. He rises and walks around the fire to the pot that sits in the coals. As he picks it up by the handle, he checks another small pot that perches on the hearthstones and says, "*Are you hungry?*"

"*No. I was, but . . . not now.*"

"*A cup of tea, perhaps?*"

"*Yes. Thank you.*"

He dips a cup into the pot hanging from the tripod at the edge of the flames and hands it to me.

"*Won't your chief be angry that I'm here, rather than in the Captives' House?*"

"*I'll risk it.*"

I drink slowly, savoring the sweet flavors of maple sap and dried cactus fruit. "*Why did you help me?*"

"You needed my help, didn't you?"

Strongheart's hand moves to my opening. He touches me lightly, and I feel him slide inside. My body reacts as Flint has trained it to, and I lunge against him.

"Don't move," he whispers. "Keep remembering that first night in Eagle Flute Village."

His voice spins out of my memories like silk. . . .

". . . Do you know why he hurt you?"

"We hurt each other for fourteen winters. Nothing has changed."

"You are the accused murderer of Chief Blue Bow. Every action Flint takes to demean you raises his status among my people. Hurting you gives him power."

Strongheart pulls the small pot from the fire, and the fragrance of soap fills the air. "I want you to tell me more, much more, but for now, I imagine you are feeling dirty."

After what I've been through, I feel filthy. . . .

He squeezes out a cloth and uses it to wash my arm. I let myself float in the sensations.

When he reaches my face, his touch becomes feather-light. He washes my forehead and around my eyes like a mother cleaning a frightened child. The cloth moves over my mouth and throat, then slips lower, cleaning my chest above my dress.

Just when I think he will slip the cloth into my dress to wash my breasts, he stops and patiently unlaces my sandals. He washes my feet. The cloth moves up my calves, and I long to lie back and fall asleep while he works.

Strongheart moved against her in a slow, leisurely rhythm, and her entire body flamed. She began moving with him. She couldn't think of anything but Strongheart now.

She opened her eyes.

Strongheart's face had turned pure gold and was fading into the light, becoming one with it.

She just barely heard him say, "Let go now. Let the light lead you into the Land of the Dead, Sora."

The glittering torrent swept her higher and higher; then it swooped downward like going over a powerful waterfall, and she was borne relentlessly toward what at first appeared to be nothing more than a tiny point of darkness. Very quickly, that point became a massive black whirlpool.

"Strongheart!" she cried, and flailed in the brilliance, fighting to swim away.

Breath rushed in and out of her lungs while the whirlpool grew larger, the blackness like nothing she had ever known. It pressed on her ears and eyes until she could neither hear nor see.

She felt herself being sucked down the ebony throat of the whirlpool and screamed.

Soundlessly.

Her cry tore from her mouth and vanished into emptiness.

She was drowning, the blackness filling up her lungs

and flooding her blood, washing away every speck of the light that had, only moments ago, permeated her body.

Out of nothingness a familiar old voice called, *"It's long past time you came to ask my advice, my daughter."*

RAIN PATTERED ON THE ROOF AND DRIPPED DOWN the smokehole, where it sizzled in the fire. The scents of wet wood and damp earth filled the chamber.

Sea Grass and Bittern had been awakened long before dawn by Tern, Bittern's daughter, who'd brought them a steaming pot of cornmeal mush for breakfast, then hastily left to take care of other duties.

Bittern clutched her bowl in her hands, eating slowly, as if greatly enjoying the dish. "I swear this is the best breakfast I've ever eaten."

Sea Grass scowled down into her bowl. "That's just because you fear it's your last. To me this tastes like it was dredged from a muck pond. What did she put in this mush?"

Bittern shrugged. "Cornmeal."

"Well, then it was moldy."

"Who cares? At least we are warm and well-fed. I didn't expect to be alive this morning."

Sea Grass glanced at her. "After Thrush and Moorhen, Wink's resolve probably evaporated. She doesn't have the stomach for murder. It's a failing that will be her ruin."

Bittern cackled suddenly. "Hallowed Ancestors, I wish I'd seen the look on Wink's face when they told her Long Fin was dead."

Sea Grass dipped another spoonful of mush, but didn't eat it. "Perhaps now she knows how I felt when Sora murdered my son. At least I have other children. Wink has no one." She ate the mush, wrinkled her nose, and set the half-empty bowl aside. Her belly had started to ache.

Bittern ate a few more bites, got a sour expression, and sniffed her mush. "You may be right; that cornmeal was moldy."

"I thought you liked it."

She dropped a hand to her stomach. "I did, but it's not sitting well. I feel like I just ate a live raccoon."

Sea Grass chuckled. "There's a racket down there, eh?"

"Yes, I . . ." The bowl dropped from Bittern's hands and cracked on one of the hearthstones. Her eyes widened. "No. It's impossible."

In panic, Sea Grass lurched to her feet. "Your daughter made this, didn't she?"

"She said she did!"

"Well, then, it can't be . . ." The cramps doubled her over.

Bittern fell to her knees and started retching as though trying to vomit up her insides.

Sea Grass sank back to the floor and stared at the doorway. She'd been expecting Feather Dancer, or perhaps Lean Elk.

She, of all people, had underestimated Wink. Now it was too late.

A low, desperate laugh shook her, and then the lethal cramps began in earnest. . . .

AN OLD WOMAN'S VOICE FILTERED THROUGH THE darkness, and images began to form. Campfires sparkled in the distance. . . . Gigantic trees thrust like black spears into the belly of the night sky. . . . A trail appeared at Sora's feet, faint and overgrown, but there.

"Mother?" she called.

She walked up the trail toward the distant campfires.

Shadows moved through the forest around her. She caught sight of pearl necklaces and pale white faces.

Footsteps stirred the grasses somewhere to her left. She spun around with her heart in her throat, trying to see through the dimness.

"Mother!" she called again. "Where are you?"

Horror gripped her when a frail old woman stepped out of the trees and onto the trail ahead. She had her gray hair pinned into a bun on top of her head and wore a silver dress that seemed made of pure moonlight. Her deeply wrinkled face gleamed with the majesty of crushed abalone shell. "What took you so long?"

Sora's throat ached with tears that her eyes could not shed. "Mother. Oh, Mother." She blurted the one thing she had always longed to say: "I didn't kill Father. I know you think I did, but he killed himself!"

She ran forward, and Chieftess Yellow Cypress turned and hobbled up the trail. No matter how hard Sora ran, her mother stayed just ahead of her.

"Mother, I need to talk with you. Wait, please wait for me?"

"Our people have been waiting for you to come here for winters, my daughter. We're tired of waiting."

Movement flickered in the trees ahead, and two ghostly forms stepped out. As her mother passed between them, she disappeared, and the white shapes drifted toward Sora with their ghostly arms out, as though to embrace her.

"Mother? Mother, come back. Help me!"

Murmuring filled the night, the ghosts speaking in a language she did not know.

"Who are you? What do you want?"

As they drifted closer, she saw the magnificent clothing they wore. Their spiderweb capes were woven so fine the delicate mesh floated. The women's faces were painted the color of fresh snow, but their eye sockets were empty and black.

They stopped a few paces in front of her and beckoned to her to step forward. Her heart shriveled.

She backed up in fear. "Tell me what you want?"

The women drifted out across the grass, toward the trees.

As though her feet understood something she refused to believe, she followed them.

Just as they entered the trees, the women evaporated like mist beneath a hot sun.

. . . And she heard a woman crying, the tears coming from deep in the chest—terrible tears that tore the souls.

Sora walked into the dark tangled forest, searching for her.

The trails were twisted and overgrown.

Finally, she ducked beneath a low-hanging branch and saw her mother sitting on a log with her arm around a young woman who was half-transparent, as though she was half here in the Land of the Dead, and half somewhere else. The woman had her head down, buried in her hands. Tears leaked between her fingers and dropped to the ground, where they rested like raindrops on the grass.

Chieftess Yellow Cypress angrily said, "She's been waiting for you for so long she's given up hope."

In confusion, Sora said, "But, who is she?"

The young woman lifted her head, and Sora stared into her own eyes.

34

THE DEEP BLUE GLEAM OF PREDAWN STREAKED the council chamber. Swirling dust motes lived in the azure shafts of light, dancing and swaying with the movements of those assembled.

Wink stood by the fire, watching the slave, Iron Hawk, dip cups of tea from the pot and deliver them to the matrons seated on three of the four benches. Twenty warriors from each clan stood around the walls. They wore worried expressions.

Voices continued to rise from the plaza outside, where the members of the Water Hickory Clan had gathered into an angry mob. News of the murders had spread throughout the night, reaching even some of the outlying villages. One hundred of Rockfish's warriors surrounded the base of Wink's mound with their war clubs clutched in tight fists. If she didn't do something soon, there would be bloodshed by sunrise.

Wink said, "First, let us all offer our condolences to Tern over the death of her mother."

Wigeon, Birch, and then Wink bowed their heads to Tern.

Enraged whispers went round the room, people speculating on who had murdered the elders of Water Hickory Clan. Most gazes pinned Wink.

"I thank you," Tern responded. Her thin face was pale and drawn, her lips pinched. She wore a beautiful ivory dress decorated with hundreds of small copper beads.

Wink lifted her voice, "And next let us welcome the new matron of Water Hickory Clan, Matron Tern."

Again, nods went round, and Tern whispered something no one could hear, but it sounded pleasant enough. She had always been a shy woman. Shy, but astute when it came to grasping political intricacies.

Birch got to her feet and said, "I would like to speak first, if that meets with the council's approval." When no one objected, Birch continued, "We have an angry mob building outside, and in a matter of days, as news of the murders spreads across our nation, there will be rioting in every Water Hickory village. I believe our main task today is to determine how to stop it. I don't want any more innocent lives—"

Wigeon drew herself up and said, "But what about the murders? Shouldn't we find the culprit first, then deal with the problems of distant villages?"

"Don't be an old fool!" Birch said. "What's more important, one murderer, or saving the lives of hundreds, maybe thousands of our people?"

Wigeon hunched as though she'd been struck in the belly. "Don't you call me a fool, Birch! I haven't ruled you out as the one who gave the orders!"

"Me?" Birch cried. "Why, you—"

"Matrons," Wink said in a loud, authoritative voice. "Let us save our accusations for later. Since Water Hickory Clan is the aggrieved party, I yield to Matron Tern." Wink sat down.

Tern looked up suddenly, her eyes wide, as though her souls had been drifting far away and had jerked back to her body when she'd heard her name. "I'm sorry, High Matron, what did you say?"

More softly, Wink repeated, "Your clan is the aggrieved party, Tern. Tell us what you think the nation's priorities should be: Should we pour our efforts into finding the murderer, or focus on calming the violence that is erupting across the Black Falcon Nation?"

Tern looked at Wink with sad eyes, and it went straight to Wink's heart.

Yes, the price of leadership is high, isn't it?

Tern inhaled a breath as though to give her strength. "I believe we must always look to the safety of our nation first. I—"

Outraged whispers came from the Water Hickory warriors leaning against the northern wall to Wink's right. Their expressions turned ugly. Feather Dancer, who stood to her left with twenty Shadow Rock warriors, straightened.

Tern was trembling, but she got to her feet and gave her warriors a piercing look that her mother would have envied. The whispers died in a heartbeat. "Matrons, please forgive my warriors. They do not yet know me." The threat in her voice was chilling. She stared at each warrior in turn. "Very soon, they will learn that I accept nothing less than absolute obedience."

Half of her warriors smirked; the other half straightened, a new respect in their eyes. Wink suspected that Tern was taking note of every smirk, and would, before nightfall, have weeded out each undesirable man.

Tern looked back at the matrons assembled on the benches; her gaze went to Wink and remained. "High Matron, I sincerely regret the difficulties caused by my clan in recent moons—"

Curses and insults rang from her warriors, and Tern whirled and pointed. "Cooter, until we know if Chief Pocket Mouse is alive or dead, you are my new war chief."

He was an ugly man with a badly pockmarked face, but twice the height of most people in the room. He squared his broad shoulders and said, "Yes, Matron."

Tern eyed the rebellious warriors. "If any other man in our clan opens his mouth, kill him."

Cooter gave her a solemn nod. "Yes, Matron."

The offensive men scowled at Cooter until he turned and glared at each one with fiery eyes. Tern had chosen well. The men went so quiet they seemed to fade into the walls.

Tern exhaled hard and hung her head for a few moments before continuing. "I am very tired, Matrons. Tired of the constant bickering between our clans, tired of making war on people I do not believe should be our enemies. Tired of death." She looked up with moist eyes. "I give you my oath that I will work very hard to correct the errors made by Matron Sea Grass and—and my mother." Saying the word hurt, for her mouth quivered before she pressed her lips tightly together. "If you will give my clan a chance."

Wink said, "Tell us what you need, Matron Tern, and we will help you all we can."

Birch and Wigeon both watched Wink with curious eyes.

Tern said, "I will dispatch messengers immediately to our village matrons and chiefs, telling them to placate their villagers until I arrive."

Birch said, "You're going to personally visit every one of the sixteen Water Hickory villages? That will take at least one moon, maybe two."

"Yes," Tern nodded. "I realize that, but I think I must sit down with each leader and talk about the future of our clan."

Wink nodded in admiration. Tern could have simply ordered every village official to meet with her in Blackbird Town, but if she went to them she had a good chance of winning their support. Support she would desperately need on the long road ahead.

Wink said, "Who will take your place in the council while you are away?"

"My daughter, Kite. I know she is young, fourteen winters, but I believe many of you ascended to leadership around that same age. When he returns from battle, I will ask my brother, Chief Pocket Mouse, to remain here as her advisor while I am gone. If that meets the council's approval."

Birch said, "I have no objections. What do you say, Wigeon? You became the matron of Shoveler Clan when you'd seen thirteen winters. Will you welcome young Kite?"

"Of course I will," Wigeon said indignantly. "But I have a question."

"Yes," Wink said.

Wigeon thrust a hand out at Tern. "I don't think she's safe wandering around the nation without a large war party. Water Hickory Clan has, in the last few days, lost most of its best warriors. Who will escort and protect her?"

Nods and whispers filtered through the room.

Birch said, "Why don't we all contribute warriors to her party? I'll offer one hundred warriors from Bald Cypress Clan."

"That's very generous, Birch," Wink said, "but there is too much fear and suspicion among our clans right now; I fear it may be dangerous for Matron Tern. I was thinking about using Rockfish's warriors. I have already spoken with War Chief Bog about helping us to suppress violence tonight. I think he would be open to this as well."

Wigeon's eyes lit up. "Yes, they are outsiders. They have no favorites among our clans. Tern, what do you think about that?"

Tern folded her hands, considering the ramifications. "Providing that I can also take twenty of my own warriors, I see no problem. I would be grateful for the help."

"How many should we send, Wink?" Birch asked.

Wink looked back at Tern. "Matron? How many warriors would you like to accompany you?"

Like a seasoned clan matron, she turned to her new war chief. "Cooter, what is your opinion?"

Cooter stepped forward, standing straight and tall. "As many as we are offered, Matron. This is not simply a matter of protecting you. Every hand that can wield a bow will add to your authority."

Tern gave him a pleased smile. "I agree with my war chief, High Matron. We would be grateful for all the help the council can give us."

Birch said, "I vote we temporarily assign all three hundred of Rockfish's warriors to serve Matron Tern."

"I agree," Wigeon said.

"As do I." Wink longed to sit down. Her legs felt weak. "Before I dismiss the council, there is another matter we must discuss."

Birch frowned. "Yes?"

Wink concentrated on keeping her face immobile

and her voice even. "The death of Chief Long Fin makes it imperative that we find a new high chief or high chieftess for the Black Falcon Nation. I will be in mourning for several days, but after that, I will be open for suggestions."

Tears filled Birch's eyes. Wigeon clamped her jaw and squinted at the fire.

Tern said, "The entire nation, including my clan, grieves with you over the loss of your son, High Matron. Water Hickory Clan is personally indebted to you for your generosity over his murder."

Wink said, "If there are no other matters to be discussed, I will dismiss this council."

No one said a word.

"I pray we all have a safe day." Wink strode for the council chamber door.

She stood outside her house in the warm flower-scented breeze while everyone filed out. Rain clouds had gathered to the south, blotting out the few remaining Star People, pushing toward Blackbird Town like a black wall.

The last to exit was Tern. She stood less than a pace from Wink, staring at her for a long time. Finally, she managed a small sad smile, and Wink smiled back, sealing the bargain that the protection of the Black Falcon Nation was passing from one woman to another—from one high matron to another.

Tern walked away surrounded by her warriors.

Feather Dancer came up beside Wink. He had one hand propped on his belted war club. With the other, he silently instructed his warriors to create a ring around Wink.

"Matron," he said, with his eyes still on the departing Water Hickory warriors, "I received word just before the council meeting that Rockfish will return this evening. He's bringing the bones of Chief Long Fin. I request permission to send a party out to meet him and escort him safely into town."

"Yes, of course. Do whatever you think is necessary, War Chief." Her vision shimmered suddenly, and she swayed on her feet.

Feather Dancer gripped her arm. "Our warriors have been straggling in throughout the night. We don't know how many survived the battle, but as they return, I will assign those still in possession of their senses to guard your house."

She nodded. "Wake me immediately if *anything* requires my attention."

"I will, Matron."

He released her arm and held the door curtain aside for her to enter the Matron's House.

She walked down the long, dimly lit corridor feeling utterly numb. Clearwing marched almost silently behind her.

If she could just get a few moments of sleep, perhaps she could stand it when Rockfish arrived.

STRONGHEART KNELT ON THE SHORE OF SAS-
safras Lake, tossing pebbles into the dark, moonlit water. Dawn was still a full hand of time away, but
anxiety knotted his belly.

Sora hadn't awakened all night. She lay curled on
her side in the lodge, lifeless. He'd felt her throat,
searching for a heartbeat, but found none. He'd placed
his ear to her chest to see if her lungs moved. Nothing.

"Oh, Sora, forgive me. I just wanted you to walk
through the doorway. I never thought it would close
behind you."

He felt as though wet strips of rawhide were drying
around his heart, squeezing the life from it. He picked
up a pebble and gripped it in a tight fist.

He had sent many people on journeys to the Land of
the Dead. All had returned. Had he done something

wrong? Perhaps he'd used too many thorn apple seeds in the tea?

"Perhaps the ghosts in the Land of the Dead wouldn't let her come home," he whispered to himself, and squinted in pain at the water. As the wind blew, moonlight glimmered from the surface.

Grief and guilt combined into a searing brew in his belly, making him sick to his stomach. "How could I have been so careless? If I've hurt her . . ."

He tossed the pebble out into the water and heard it splash. A sleeping goose honked in surprise.

He watched silently as the goose paddled closer. She murmured to him and tilted her head first to the left, then to the right, as though asking him a question he was too obtuse to understand.

"I don't understand, my sister. I wish I did."

The goose peered over his shoulder, at the lodge, then turned and paddled away, heading out into the middle of the lake, where three other geese slept, bobbing gently on the water.

Strongheart frowned, and turned toward the lodge. The soft breeze tousled the thatch, and Sister Moon's gleam shone from the freshly cut saplings, but he saw nothing unusual. He looked back out at the four geese. They appeared to be sleeping again, their bills tucked securely beneath their wings. He'd reached for another pebble when he heard a low sound coming from the lodge.

A weak voice called, "Strongheart?"

He spun around with his eyes wide. "*Sora!*"

He ran and ducked beneath the door curtain into the dark lodge. The fire had burned down to red glowing eyes of coals, casting a carnelian gleam over the walls and her pale beautiful face. She lay propped on one elbow. Long black hair spilled around her naked body in a glistening wealth.

"Blessed gods," Strongheart said, "I'm glad to see you. I was afraid I'd—"

"I found her," she said faintly, and gazed at him so steadily he saw the flickering coals reflected in her eyes.

"Who?"

A cool lake-scented breeze blew through the lodge, fanning the coals to a crimson hue. Sparks crackled up and lazily spiraled toward the smokehole.

"Who did you find, Sora?"

She blinked and slowly, as though with difficulty, said, "My reflection-soul. I found her in the forest. My mother was with her."

"Did she speak with you?"

"Yes, she . . ." The word faded to nothingness, and her dark eyes fixed on the doorway, seeing something not in this world. "She told me the pitiful cries never stopped. She had to leave. She was going insane."

"I understand."

As though she hadn't heard, she continued, "Every time she comes home, they start again. She can't stand it."

He cocked his head. Her eyes had gone vacant, as though her shadow-soul was, even now, walking in the Land of the Dead, seeing the faces of long-lost ancestors.

"Did you speak with your mother?"

She nodded. "Mother has been caring for my reflection-soul for many winters. Every time my reflection-soul flees to the Land of the Dead, Mother finds her and comforts her."

"That's probably why you're still alive. Your mother keeps talking her into returning to this world. Most people in your circumstances would have died—"

"I told her I didn't kill Father," she choked out, and tears filled her eyes. "But she already knew."

He reached out and smoothed a hand over her silken hair. "Yes, at death, all things are made clear. What else did you tell her?"

"I told her I was sorry I hadn't caught her the day she fell." She wiped the tears from her cheeks with one hand.

"Did she forgive you?"

"She told me that she'd never blamed me for her death. She . . ." Emotion welled in her voice, cutting off her breath. She swallowed and continued, "I asked her about the cries."

A mosquito flew through the gap in the door curtain and buzzed around her head, catching her eye. She watched it for a time before saying, "Mother told me to stop being foolish, that every night I knew where the cries were coming from, and every morning I refused to remember it."

Strongheart sank to the floor as though the wind had

been knocked out of him. A hollow pounding began in his chest and spread through his body. "Did you understand what she meant?"

The answer had been there all along, right in front of her eyes. He wondered if she could see it now.

Tears welled in her eyes and drained down her cheeks. "Yes. I know who the ghost person is."

Strongheart touched her hand and said, "Sleep now. I know how exhausting a Spirit journey can be. Sleep, Sora."

IN THE CERULEAN GLEAM JUST AFTER DUSK, SORA woke to find Strongheart lying beside her with his head propped on his hand, watching her. His short black hair had fallen forward, fringing his forehead.

"A pleasant evening to you," he said. His eyes shone with a strange warm light.

Wind flapped the door curtain, revealing glimpses of Sassafras Lake, and the mist that lay in gossamer clouds around the trunks of the trees. She pulled the blanket up around her throat. "It's chilly."

"Yes, rain fell most of the day."

"You were up all night and all day?"

He smiled. "I needed time to think."

She noticed that Flint's war club leaned against the wall beside the door and his stiletto rested on the floor above Strongheart's head. Sometime during the day

Strongheart had untied them from their belt and left them in strategic locations, just in case he needed to protect her.

She said, "About how to cure me?"

His dark eyes were kind as he heard the winters of buried desperation leak into her voice. "No, I was thinking about the future."

"You mean what happens after you've cured me."

Gently, he said, "Sora, you *are* cured."

"What do you mean?"

He smiled forlornly. "Tell me what you would like to do for the rest of your life?"

As the Cloud People shifted, starlight flashed on the lake, then vanished, veiling the world in gray again. "I just want to go home."

"And take up where you left off?"

"No. I can't do that. Long Fin is high chief of the Black Falcon Nation now. Wink has been grooming him to be chief all of his life. I won't take it away from him."

"But if you are not chieftess, what will you do?"

She ran a hand through her long, tangled hair. "Maybe I'll go home, barricade my bedchamber door, and sit by the fire for a few moons. Which, of course, sounds ridiculous."

He trailed his fingers down her arm, and she heaved a deep sigh. His touch had become the heart of her world.

"It doesn't sound ridiculous," he said. "There are times when I wish I were back in Forbidden Village with Juggler. Life was simpler when it was just the two of us."

"And safer," she said as she once again looked out the doorway. Some nagging sound out there made her uneasy. Like the distant hiss of voices . . . though it was probably the rain falling through the branches.

Strongheart reached up and smoothed her hair off her shoulder. His tender touch made her shiver. "You are safer now than you have been in many winters, Sora."

"I don't feel safe."

"I don't mean from the outside world. I mean from what lives inside you."

For a time gray veils of mist blew by the doorway like twisting scarves, fluttering the curtain and filling the lodge with the scent of the lake. Strongheart stared at her, and she saw her own reflection in his dark eyes. It was a shock. Where once a beautiful woman would have looked back, now she saw a tired and ghastly pale version of herself.

"You mean you killed the Midnight Fox?"

He shook his head lightly. "No, the Fox is still there; you just don't have to worry about him now."

She pulled away, almost angrily, and said, "Don't say things like that unless you plan to explain them."

His smile faded, and she felt shaken by his gaze. He sat up and leaned over her, as though to make certain she was looking straight at him when he said, "For many winters, the Midnight Fox has kept guard over the child. It's been his sole purpose. Last night we—"

Strongheart jerked around to stare at the door.

Then she heard them.

Steps pounded up the shore, running, and there was more than one man.

ROCKFISH LEANED FORWARD ON THE BENCH AND propped his elbows on his knees. Wink sat a few hands away, staring at the leather-wrapped bundle that rested on the bench between them. Her eyes were tight, but dry. The flickering torchlight showed the exhaustion in her face. The lines across her forehead cut much deeper now than one moon ago.

Wink put a hand over the bundle, as though to touch her son. "You did well, Rockfish. The Black Falcon Nation appreciates your service."

"It was my honor to serve."

He grimaced at the sacred masks on the walls before asking, "What do you think of the new Water Hickory matron, Tern?"

"She's starting out well. She seems truly dedicated to the survival of the Black Falcon Nation." Wink smoothed her hand over the bundle. "She understands the terrible mistakes made by her former clan elders."

Rockfish tucked a dirty strand of white hair behind his ear. He'd been running hard since the battle, trying to get back to Blackbird Town with Long Fin's bones. Mud spattered his tan shirt and red leggings. "Did you . . . ?" he started, then stopped. He wasn't sure he really wanted to know.

"Did I what?"

"The rumors flying down the trails are that you personally murdered the Water Hickory elders."

"No," she answered. "I didn't."

Relieved, Rockfish said, "Thank the gods, but if you didn't do it . . ."

Wink patted the bundle and drew her hand back to her lap. She straightened her spine and looked at him with cold, tired eyes. "Rockfish, do you understand the Black Falcon Law of Retribution?"

He shrugged. "It seems simple enough. If I were to kill a member of your clan, you would have the right to claim my life or the life of a member of my clan."

"Yes, that's right."

When she didn't go on, his bushy white brows drew together.

Long Fin?

"Are you saying that because Water Hickory warriors killed your son, you claimed the life of someone in their clan? Matron Sea Grass?"

"No, not Sea Grass. I claimed the life of Tern's daughter, Kite." Wink pulled her gaze from his and stared sightlessly at the fire. "I claimed her life in advance."

"I don't understand."

Through a tired exhalation she said, "You wouldn't. You aren't of our people."

Rockfish thought about it. "Do you mean you . . . ?" He blinked as the implications came into focus. "You went to Tern before you decided to send Chief Long Fin with the war party? That you told Tern that if Water Hickory killed him, you would—"

In a strained voice, she interrupted, "Yes."

That raised a series of disturbing questions. Wink was a master politician. Had she played out every possible outcome in her souls, and finally understood that the death of her son was the only way to keep the nation together? And she . . .

Rockfish asked, "Kite has seen barely fourteen winters. Why would you choose her?"

"I knew Tern would bargain for her daughter's life. Someday soon, Tern will rule the Black Falcon Nation as the high matron, and her daughter will be high chieftess. Of course, I had to explain it to her. She has a few obstacles to overcome."

Rockfish leaned back on the bench and blinked in amazement. "Dear gods, when that day comes the Water Hickory Clan will have more power than it ever dreamed of."

Wink massaged her forehead. "Yes, providing Tern has a nation to rule. I told her that civil war would shatter

the nation and probably be the death of Water Hickory
Clan. She genuinely loves the Black Falcon Nation. She
knew what she had to do."

What she had to do . . . dear gods.

Rockfish softly said, "As you did."

Wink's eyes just tightened.

He sat unmoving for a time, then rose to his feet.
"Has there been any word of my wife? Was she killed
in the Eagle Flute Village massacre?"

As though it broke her heart, Wink's voice went
deathly quiet: "I heard a rumor from an unreliable
source, Rockfish. Are you sure you wish to hear it? It
may make things worse for you."

"Tell me, Wink." Despite the age difference between
them, he'd genuinely loved Sora. If she was dead, he
needed to know. Only then could he start healing his
world. "Please."

Wink nodded. "I heard that she was being held north
of Minnow Village."

"Held? By whom?"

Wink looked at the floor, and her brows lifted. "Two
men. Priest Strongheart and Flint."

Rockfish let his weary souls absorb that before he
said, "I assume you've already dispatched a search
party?"

"No search party, Rockfish. I believed, and still believe, that sending out a large party will only attract attention in these desperate times."

A knot formed in his throat. She was probably right.

There were too many war parties scouring the forests. A large party would almost certainly be attacked. But he had to know. . . .

"I thank you for telling me. Once I've rested, I'll go myself."

"Alone?"

"Yes." He got to his feet. "Before I go find my blankets, there's one last thing you must know."

"Yes?"

"Before Long Fin died, he asked me to tell you he was sorry."

She frowned in confusion. "Sorry?"

"Yes, he wanted you to know that he was sorry for being a bad chief."

The sob caught in her throat. She closed her eyes and turned away so that Rockfish couldn't see her face.

When her shoulders began to shake, he hesitated. In less than one half moon, Wink had lost everyone important to her: her best friend Sora, and now her only child.

Rockfish started to go to her, and Wink thrust out a hand, and said, "No, please, just go."

His heart might have been stone as he left her chamber.

38

Soft male laughter drifted from the forest as the steps came closer, splashing in the puddles, as though the men did not care who heard them.

"Get up," Strongheart said. "Quickly."

He grabbed her dress and threw it at her, then slipped his brown shirt over his head. "There's no time to waste. I'll try to delay them while you get away."

He lunged for the door, but just before he ducked out, a fist slammed into his chest, knocking him backward into the lodge. Strongheart rolled, grabbed for the war club propped against the wall, and came up swinging. He caught the first man squarely across the chest. She heard ribs snap as he toppled forward into the lodge. "Run!" Strongheart shouted at her.

Sora leaped over the fallen man, raced through the

door, and out into the darkness. Rain poured from the sky, battering the tree limbs and soaking her dress.

As she fled, a warrior dashing up the shore saw her, pulled an arrow from his quiver and, with trained and deadly speed, nocked it in his bow. He fought to aim on the run, and she feinted a lunge for a hickory tree, then dove in the opposite direction. The arrow cracked against the hickory trunk and splintered wood spun through the air.

Heart hammering, she plunged across a small swampy bog and ran headlong for—

A hand shot out from behind a cypress trunk, swiped at her arm, missed, and grabbed hold of her dress. The warrior wrenched with all his might, jerking her off her feet. She landed hard, and the skinny youth fell upon her growling like a wolf.

"Rail! I caught her!" he yelled.

"Good," Rail called. "Hold her!"

Another man stepped from the brush with his war lance held at the ready. When he saw her, he instinctively stepped back. "Osprey, that's Chieftess Sora! Blessed gods, Flint was telling the truth!"

Osprey blinked the rain from his eyes and scrutinized her. "Are you sure, Snipe? I don't think it's her."

"Yes, it is, you fool! You're just used to seeing her dressed in finery and covered with rare jewels!"

Rail trotted up and gasped, "Is it—"

"Yes," Snipe said. "It's her. And you almost killed her! Flint is not going to be happy."

Sora roared, "Release me, or I'll have your heads!"

They dragged her to her feet and shoved her back toward the lodge. Snipe prodded her with his spear to keep her walking.

Long before they got there, she saw a tall broad-shouldered man striding up the shore with a shapely young woman at his side. Both wore black capes. Her heart ached. Over the eighteen winters she had loved Flint, his every move had been etched on her souls: the way he walked, waved his hands, laughed, wept. He was part of her in a way no man would ever be again.

Flint didn't even look at her. He told the woman, "Stay here," then strode up to Rail and thrust his stiletto between the man's ribs.

Stunned, Rail groaned and released Sora's arm. He staggered before he sat down hard, his wide disbelieving eyes on Flint. "What did . . . I do?"

Flint bent over, and rain poured from his hood. "I saw you nock your bow and chase her down the shore. I told you *not* to kill her."

Rail let out a breath that might have been a laugh as he toppled to his side in a pool of rainwater.

Flint straightened and stared hard into the eyes of the other two warriors; they shifted uneasily. In a deadly voice, he ordered, "Bring her."

39

FLINT SHOVED SORA TO THE GROUND OUTSIDE THE new lodge and started pacing back and forth with his black cape blowing around his tall body. He wore a frail, devastated expression, as though his entire world had dissolved before his eyes. "I told you I'd find you," he said in a shaking voice. "Didn't you believe me?"

The unknown woman, young, with a haughty expression on her beautiful face, stood by watching. A thick black braid fell over her left shoulder. Obviously a warrior, she carried a war club in her hand. Even in the darkness, the freshly dried blood shone on her tan leggings.

To her right Sora saw a blur of motion as the two other men bodily hauled Strongheart to a pine tree, where they ripped off their belts, wrenched his arms around the trunk, and tied them. Then they tied his feet, and grunts sounded as fists met flesh.

"Flint," Sora pleaded, "stop this! You don't know what you're doing! You—"

"Shut your mouth, camp bitch!" the young woman shouted.

When Sora tried to get to her feet, the woman kicked her down hard and kept her sandal pressed into the middle of Sora's back, growling, "Flint knows very well what he's doing. He always does!"

The bizarre statement made Sora twist her head around to look at the woman. "Who are you?"

The woman gave her a grisly smile and leaned down to say, "*I'm* the woman Flint loves."

From the tree where he was tied, Strongheart called, "You're White Fawn, aren't you?"

Sora's gaze darted back to the woman, and a sick dizzy sensation filled her.

"Yes," the woman laughed. "Are you surprised that I'm not dead?"

White Fawn . . . I didn't kill her. . . .

Flint slipped an arm around White Fawn's shoulders and hugged her. "Yes, White Fawn is the new hero of our nation. The right hand of soon-to-be High Matron Sea Grass."

"Right hand?" Strongheart asked. "Because she killed Chief Short Tail? She's an assassin, nothing more."

Sora stared open-mouthed at Flint. "Short Tail? Wh-who else has she killed?"

"Far Eye, for one. And the boy chief, what was his name?" Flint asked mockingly.

White Fawn said, "Long Fin."

Sora's souls seemed to lift out of her body and fly away into the darkness. A hollow ache spread through her. She whispered, "Why?"

Flint shrugged. "He was Wink's son." He proudly hugged White Fawn again. She smiled up at him in absolute adoration.

Sora had once smiled at him that same way. A curious pity filled her—pity for White Fawn and the life she had to look forward to as Flint's wife.

Strongheart called, "When Water Hickory Clan rules the Black Falcon Nation you will be the new war chief, won't you, Flint? Isn't that your reward for betraying the high chieftess?"

Flint laughed, "That and more."

Sora cried, "Your clan will never—!"

Flint kicked her over and fell upon her like a starving wolf. She slammed her fists into his face and shoulders, but he grabbed her wrists, pinned them over her head, and said, "White Fawn, hold her hands."

White Fawn knelt, tied her war club to her belt, and grabbed Sora's hands, totally unperturbed, as though she'd seen him rape a hundred women.

"Flint, let Strongheart go!" Sora ordered. "This is between you and me."

"Oh, yes, I know." He jerked her dress up and shoved her legs apart. While she struggled, he pulled his shirt over his hips. He was staring into her eyes when he viciously drove himself into her. A hoarse cry tore her throat.

Strongheart struggled against his bonds, shouting, "Flint, stop it! Hurt me, not her!"

Snipe, the younger of the two warriors, walked up beside Flint and leaned on his war lance to watch. More slowly, Osprey broke away from Strongheart and trotted over. In less than twenty heartbeats, their manhoods thrust against their war shirts. White Fawn didn't even seem to notice.

Snipe licked his lips and glanced at Osprey. "How long does it take him? Have you warred with him before?"

Osprey shrugged. "I don't know."

Flint smiled at Osprey, then withdrew and stood up. The two men squinted at him as though they couldn't believe he hadn't finished.

Flint rubbed his mouth with the back of his hand and gestured to Sora. "She's not ready for me yet. Osprey, why don't you try?"

Sora wrenched against White Fawn's iron grip, but couldn't break free. No emotion played on Flint's face. No regret. No sympathy.

Blessed gods, how long has he hated me?

Osprey's young eyes widened. He couldn't have seen more than eighteen winters. "Me? You want me to get her ready for you?"

"Yes. Or are you too much of a boy to do it?"

"I'll show you who is a boy."

Osprey rushed to shed his cape and untie his breech-clout. When he crawled on top of Sora, the stench of his stale sweat almost gagged her. In less than five heartbeats, he'd forced himself inside and let out a deep-throated groan of pleasure.

"Great Spirits, she holds a man like a fist! You told me, but I didn't believe you!"

As Snipe watched Osprey working himself into a frenzy, he started to swallow convulsively. "I know you promised us each a turn, but I didn't think I'd want one. She's our chieftess, a forbidden woman."

When Osprey started panting and groaning, Snipe gripped Flint's arm. "You won't tell anyone I took her, will you? No matter what happens, if High Matron Wink ever found out—"

Flint shook off his hand. "For the sake of the gods, you're a coward! Wink doesn't rule the entire world. Besides, she will soon be dead." He looked at White Fawn, and she nodded.

Osprey bit Sora's neck hard, and she cried out as warm blood trickled down her throat. Her cry excited Osprey even more. He laughed and slammed against her.

Snipe stared at Flint with wide eyes. "Is that who White Fawn is supposed to kill next? High Matron Wink?"

"Of course," White Fawn answered. "If I hadn't gotten caught up in the battle at Fan Palm Village, she'd have been dead two days ago."

Osprey cried out and went limp on top of Sora. His heavy breathing made her want to retch. Flint kicked Osprey and said, "Get off."

Osprey rolled off her and got to his feet.

"Snipe," Flint said. "Do it quickly or don't do it at all."

Snipe made an awkward gesture with his war lance. "You finish first, Flint, while I decide."

"While you decide if you're brave enough?" Flint said sarcastically, and stretched out on top of Sora again. "Are you ready for me now, my former wife?"

Sora closed her eyes against the pain. His thrusts were the motions of a careless stranger. He wanted to hurt her.

"Flint," she whispered, "what's this about? This punishment is more than—"

"Wink has allied Shadow Rock Clan with our enemies. We lost many friends yesterday."

"Allied . . . with our enemies?" Her souls rapidly began putting together every shred of information she knew. "Wink allied Shadow Rock Clan with the Loon Nation? Is that what happened? And—and you were you in a battle? Water Hickory Clan was in a battle at Fan Palm Village? A battle it lost?"

He pounded against her, and she saw Snipe's hand lower to his erect penis.

"Hurry, Flint," he said in a constricted voice.

Flint gripped her breasts, squeezing them hard enough to leave bruises while he lunged against her. "I don't want you to ever forget me, Sora," he whispered in her ear. "I'm the man who brought you and your clan down."

"Flint, please, let me—"

When Flint cried out and collapsed on top of her, Snipe tossed his war lance down and ripped off his breechclout. "Is it my turn?"

Flint rose and smoothed his wet war shirt down. Rain beaded his face as he lifted it to scan the brightening sky. The clouds had broken. Stars glittered in the dark blue gaps, and silver shafts of light pierced the forest.

White Fawn released Sora's hands and rose. "What about the priest?"

Flint didn't even look at her; he just strode for where Strongheart was tied to the tree.

Snipe begged, "White Fawn, can you hold her hands for me? Please?"

White Fawn sneered, kicked Snipe's lance aside, and grabbed Sora's hands again. "Get on with it. There's no telling who's going to come stumbling in here. It could be our side or theirs. If it's her side, we'll all be dead."

Snipe brutally kissed her and slid inside. She twisted her head away . . . and looked straight at Strongheart.

As Flint approached, Strongheart quietly said, "There are so many things you can't forgive yourself for. This will be another."

"I told you to stop trying to Heal me!" Flint shouted. "I don't need you!"

Strongheart stared at him with starlit eyes. Rain had drenched his shirt, making it stick to his tall body like a second skin. "Did you tell her the story about Walking Bird, or was that staged?"

Flint frowned. "Was what staged?"

Strongheart's eyes narrowed, and he seemed to be winnowing out truth from falsehood. "Maybe it wasn't you, but your lover, Skinner."

White Fawn's head jerked up. She frowned at Flint. "Your lover? What's he talking about?"

Flint seemed to shrink, his shoulders hunching as though to protect himself from a blow. "Stop this, Priest, before you force me to—"

"Where were you the night he died? Why weren't you in the forest watching? You watched them every other time, didn't you?"

White Fawn said, "Flint, what does he mean? About you and Skinner?"

Flint squeezed his eyes closed, and Sora saw his fists shaking. "I warned you, Priest."

In an absolutely silent move, Flint pulled his stiletto from his belt, stepped forward, and plunged it into Strongheart's chest.

Once, twice.

Sora screamed, and Snipe laughed in her ear and pumped harder.

Blood pulsed from Strongheart's wounds in time with his heartbeat, draining down his chest and splattering his legs. In a quaking voice, Strongheart asked, "Were you meeting with . . . your matron? Arranging . . . Sora's death?"

Flint wiped his stiletto off on his shirt and tucked it

back in his belt. He walked to Sora, standing over her, as Snipe stiffened and moaned.

Strongheart sagged against the tree, and Sora started weeping.

In a wrathful voice, Flint leaned over her and asked, "Do you miss him?"

When she just sobbed, Flint waved to Osprey, "Come back over here."

Osprey trotted forward. "What is it? What do you want?"

Flint ordered, "Pull off your breechclout. We're going to take her again."

"But, Flint, I—I don't think I—"

Flint shouted, "You are boys! Both of you! Get out of my way!"

Flint kicked Snipe hard in the ribs, and the youth grunted and scrambled off Sora.

"Watch how a man does this," Flint shouted.

Osprey and Snipe moved closer, and Flint fell upon Sora like a rabid dog, snarling and biting.

40

FLINT DRAGGED THE PANTING SNIPE TO HIS FEET and shoved him hard in the direction of the lake. "Now go guard the trails. Both of you! Signal me if you hear anyone coming."

"Yes, Flint." Snipe tied on his breechclout while he hurried south after Osprey.

White Fawn released Sora's hands and stared at Flint in a way that obviously made him uncomfortable. He shouted, "Stop looking at me like that!"

White Fawn lowered her gaze, and Sora rolled to her side. Through blurry eyes she saw Strongheart. His head hung limply.

"We should tie her up and be on our way to Blackbird Town," White Fawn said stiffly. "I have a duty to perform."

"Yes, you're right. Sora, get on your feet."

A curious light-headed sensation swept her. She sat up. "I'm not going anywhere with you."

"Oh, yes, you are. We need you. At least until Wink is dead."

At the mention of Wink's name, Sora went rigid. "Are you planning on using me against her?"

As though speaking to a five-winters-old child, Flint said, "You are the best weapon we have. That's why you're still alive."

Flint bent down, grabbed her by the wrist, and hauled her to her feet. "You're the perfect bait. We'll tell Wink we're holding you just outside of Blackbird Town. All she has to do is come alone and we'll turn you over, in exchange for a fortune in pearls or fabrics, or whatever I deem appropriate at the time." He jerked his chin at White Fawn, and ordered, "Find something to tie Sora's hands."

White Fawn looked around, then marched over to the tree where Strongheart sagged and began untying the cord around his legs.

Sora whispered, "Flint . . . where were you the night Skinner died?"

He flicked a hand to dismiss the question. "You don't want to know, believe me."

"I *do* want to know."

He dragged her close and, with his mouth almost touching hers, whispered, "Matron Wood Fern ordered me to her chamber."

He was betraying me. . . .

"Were you helping her lay the plans to get me to Eagle Flute Village?"

He put a hand around her throat and squeezed. "Yes, it was a stroke of brilliance. The Loon People would almost certainly kill you for the death of Blue Bow, and no one could blame us. The Law of Retribution would be fulfilled without Water Hickory Clan ever lifting a finger." He smiled and let his hand fall.

She stood there, shaking all over, looking into Flint's eyes, but she didn't really see him. Just over his shoulder she could see Strongheart. His dark eyes were no longer luminous, but dull and still.

Sora's breathing turned to spasmodic sobbing.

Flint grabbed her shoulders and spun her around so she couldn't see Strongheart. "He's dead. Let's go."

"Just let me touch him one last time. I need to—"

"No, Sora!"

Flint flung her forward into a shambling trot . . . just as a last breath escaped Strongheart's lungs.

Instinctively, White Fawn leapt back, and Flint jerked his war club from his belt and whirled around as though to defend her.

The world seemed to slow down, every moment dragging by. . . .

As though it didn't belong to her, Sora watched her own hand reach for the stiletto tucked in Flint's belt, pull it free, and plunge it into his throat. Blood gushed from the wound.

From somewhere far away, she heard White Fawn scream.

Flint swayed on his feet, blinked, then laughed softly as he touched the blood draining down his neck. He shook his head in disbelief. "Sora . . . you always surprise me." He staggered and dropped to his knees.

"Flint!" White Fawn ran to him. She pressed her hands over the hole as though to stop the blood, and cried, "No, no, no! You whore! What have you done?"

Flint coughed and toppled backward, his body twisting in impossible contortions while he wheezed like a drowning man. The entire time he was writhing, he stared straight into Sora's eyes. Stared at her until his body began to relax, and his limbs ceased twitching.

When he finally lay still, White Fawn stumbled to her feet, breathing hard. "You killed him. You killed my Flint."

She turned toward Sora, and her gaze dropped to Sora's hand.

Sora looked down. She'd forgotten she still held the stiletto.

White Fawn glanced at the war club tied on her belt and seemed to be calculating whether or not she could untie it before Sora was upon her.

"Don't do it," Sora warned. "I don't want to have to kill you!"

"You? Kill *me?*"

Screaming in rage, White Fawn leapt for Sora, knocked her to the ground, and grabbed the hand that held the stiletto. While they rolled across the muddy shore, grunting, struggling for the upper hand, White Fawn shrieked, "Snipe! Osprey! Where are you? Snipe! *Osprey!*" She looked dazed, on the verge of madness.

Sora landed a fist to White Fawn's temple and, momentarily stunned, the woman's grip on the stiletto eased. Sora ripped it free and stabbed White Fawn in the chest. Her fear-charged muscles couldn't seem to stop. She stabbed the woman over and over and over . . .

Until a man's hand reached out of the darkness, grabbed hers, and forcibly stopped her.

In terror she fought against him, screaming, not even bothering to look at his face.

"Chieftess!" Lean Elk said as he knelt at her side and tugged the stiletto away. A tall man with dark, oddly inhuman eyes, he wore a brown shirt. "She's dead."

"No, no, sh-she might not—"

"She's *dead.* I give you my oath." He tossed the stiletto into the forest, then looked her straight in the eyes and said, "I killed the other two men, but there are more Water Hickory warriors coming. Please, we have barely enough to time to get away."

He pulled her to her feet and stared at her. "Did you hear me, Chieftess?"

An ache grew in her heart, as though she were, once again, being sucked down into that gigantic black whirlpool that led to the Land of the Dead. Somewhere deep inside her, a voice kept repeating, *Strongheart is dead, Strongheart is dead, Strongheart is dead.*

On weak legs, she walked to the tree where he was

tied, and gently lifted his head. Through blurry eyes she stared at him, remembering the tenderness of his touch, his smile, the warmth in his eyes. She wrapped her arms around him and buried her face in the fabric over his shoulder. Barely audible, she wept, "Forgive me. Forgive me for needing you so much."

"Please hurry, Chieftess." Lean Elk gestured to the trail, then turned and trotted into the forest.

She closed her eyes for a long moment, then released Strongheart and forced her legs to move, to follow Lean Elk.

41

She'd been trotting through the forest for over four hands of time when her legs gave out and she stumbled and almost fell before she caught herself. "Please, Lean Elk," she called, "give me a few moments."

He stopped and turned. Silhouetted against the dark oaks, he was almost invisible. "Of course, my Chieftess, but we mustn't stay long."

She sank to the ground, and Lean Elk pulled his ceramic canteen from his belt and carried it over to her. As he removed the wooden stopper, he said, "Drink a little, but not too much."

She took the canteen and sipped it. The cool water burned a path down her raw throat. "Thank you."

He knelt in front of her, and his gaze took in her

trembling limbs. "You know I wouldn't be pushing so hard if it weren't necessary, don't you?"

"Yes. I know." She took three more sips and handed the canteen to him. As he drank, she asked, "How did you know I was in Forbidden Village?"

"Matron Wink. She told me to run fast, but she knew only that you were somewhere north of Minnow Village. It's a miracle I found you as quickly as I did." He gave her a small proud smile. "I should have known you wouldn't really need me, my chieftess."

Wink.

She had always been there during the darkest moments of Sora's life, loving her, fighting for her with blind, passionate loyalty against Flint and against Sora's mother and so many others, even battling their own clan when necessary.

She pulled her shoulders back and said, "What's happening in Blackbird Town?" When he tried to avoid her gaze, she ordered, "Look at me. I asked you what was happening at home. Tell me."

Reluctantly, he answered, "When I left, two days ago, Matron Wink was in trouble."

"What kind of trouble?"

He hesitated, and it occurred to her that Wink had probably sworn him to secrecy.

She said, "It's all right, Lean Elk, you can tell me. She would want you to."

He nodded, but swallowed hard before he said, "Our matron summoned me in the middle of the night. She had just ordered the death of Red Raven, and—"

"Good, the little weasel was a traitor. What else?"

"Elder Moorhen had just been murdered."

Sora blinked. Moorhen was a cranky, evil old woman, always plotting behind Wink's back. Had Wink finally had enough? "Who killed her? You?"

He shook his head vigorously. "No. I swear it. I don't know who the assassin was."

Her hands clenched to fists as she gazed out at the forest. Starlight draped the branches like handfuls of gleaming pewter scarves. While Wink might be cleaning house, eliminating her adversaries, Sora didn't think so. It was too dangerous to kill the elders of a rival clan. Wink wouldn't make such a mistake. Unless she'd had no other choice.

She wouldn't do it unless she believed the entire Black Falcon Nation was about crumble before her eyes. Is it?

It was as though her shattered reflection-soul suddenly coalesced, the pieces melding together into a perfect whole. She could see everything with a strange clarity.

She rose on shaking legs. "Let's go home."

He nodded, got to his feet, and led the way up the trail.

She swiftly broke into a trot.

For the first time in over a moon, she knew exactly where she was going and what she had to do.

42

DOGWOOD PETALS, BLOWN FROM THE TREES BY last night's ferocious wind, covered the ground and bobbed across the vast expanse of Persimmon Lake like tiny boats.

Rockfish watched them from where he sat on a log bench at the edges of the chunkey field. Birch and Wigeon sat to his right and Wink to his left. Everyone wore their finest clothing. His own shirt, a saffron-colored garment covered with whelk-shell fetishes, glistened like a rainbow.

After Matron Birch had organized the chunkey game, people had come from everywhere to attend the feast in honor of Chief Long Fin. Birch, wisely, had specified that the contest would be between Bald Cypress Clan and Shoveler Clan, but warriors from the other clans lined the edges of the field.

A cheer went up, and Rockfish looked in time to see the spear arcing downward toward the slowly rolling chunkey stone. The spear landed right next to the stone as it toppled.

"Bald Cypress earns another point!" Birch said proudly. "Two more points and we'll win this game; then we can uncover the stew pots and feast."

Wigeon said, "You're not going to win. We are. You're just ahead of us for the time being."

"Well, we'll see about that." Birch grinned at Wigeon.

Rockfish almost groaned when yet another dignitary from a distant village came forward and knelt to touch his forehead to Wink's sandals. She looked utterly exhausted, her round face sunken and pale. Rockfish thought he recognized the dignitary, but wasn't sure.

The man said, "I grieve with you over the loss of your son, High Matron. All the people of Slipper Shell Village send their condolences."

Slipper Shell Village, of course. He's from the Sandhill Crane People.

Wink smiled and put a hand on his head to signal him to rise. "The Black Falcon Nation thanks you, Chief Mangrove. I thank you." She gestured to the game. "Please, enjoy yourself."

He rose, bowed, and walked away.

Matron Birch leaned sideways and told Wink, "Don't worry, you've seen almost everyone now."

"Thank the gods. This gauntlet of sympathy is almost too much to bear. I wish I—"

Wink stopped so suddenly that Rockfish turned to look at her. Her hand had risen to her throat, clutching it as though it ached, and he could see the tears well in her eyes.

He grabbed her arm. "Wink, are you all right? What—"

In an instant, she threw off his hand and was on her feet, running.

Rockfish shielded his eyes from the glare of the sun. Two people had just rounded the curve in the trail and were headed for the plaza. Both the man and woman wore filthy rags, and long braids hung over their shoulders.

Birch said, "Probably latecomers to the feast."

"Dressed like that?" Wigeon said. "I hope not. It's disrespectful."

As the two women ran into each other's arms and their joyous cries rose, Rockfish's wrinkled face slackened.

"Oh, blessed gods, it's Sora!"

He leaped to his feet.

43

WINK SAT ON A MAT IN SORA'S BEDCHAMBER AND watched the woman who had been her best friend for more than twenty-five winters. Sora knelt in front of the fire adding branches to the blaze. She had slept, bathed, and pinned her long black hair back with tortoiseshell combs. The style made her pointed nose seem longer, her high cheekbones more severe. Worse, her black eyes looked huge and empty. As though sick to her stomach, she kept wiping her hands on her purple dress and swallowing.

Wink had seen her enraged, in despair, and brokenhearted, but this was something different. Sora was alien in a way Wink couldn't yet define.

Her gaze scanned the room, moving over the two copper-covered wooden celts, ceremonial clubs, that hung side by side over the hide-covered sleeping bench. They had belonged to Sora's mother. Beneath the sleeping bench, she saw the corner of the wooden box where Sora kept her ritual jewels, and to the left of the bench stood Sora's clothing basket. Everything looked exactly as she remembered.

But a somber, frightening wrongness lived and breathed in the walls. Wink could feel it lurking there, waiting for something, but she did not know what. No matter how she tried to shake it, that eerie sensation of disaster to come persisted.

Wink tried to shake if off. She said, "I have something for you," and smiled as she pulled the pendant from around her own throat.

"What is it?"

Wink walked over to where Sora knelt on the mat by the fire and extended the gorget, the necklace. "The little boy, Touches Clouds, asked me to give this to you. He said he was cured, and wanted you to have it back."

Sora had given it to the sick boy just before Flint had taken her to Eagle Flute Village.

Sora took the large circular rattlesnake pendant and stared down into its one huge eye. Carved from a conch shell, the stylized serpent coiled back and forth, forming spirals around its central eye. "Brilliant lookers," they were called, because their bright unblinking eyes had the power to kill. Priests coiled enormous spiritual snakes around the houses of sick people to keep away Raven Mockers, the most dangerous witches, leaving only a narrow space between the head and tail for relatives to enter and exit.

Priest Teal had given this Brilliant Looker to Sora three winters ago, right after Flint divorced her. He'd told Sora it would protect her against Flint's witchcraft. *She should never have taken it off.*

"You know, I almost didn't recognize you when I saw you this morning," Wink said.

"Lean Elk led me down some tortuous trails to get home. There were warriors everywhere. We had to run almost straight through."

Wink reached out to touch her hand, and softly said, "I missed you very much."

Sora took her hand and held it tightly. "As I missed you. How is everything in Blackbird Town?"

"Oh, I think that for now, we're all right. Over the next few days, I'll explain all of the political details to you."

"Good. I want to know everything. Especially everything about Tern. I understand she attended her first council meeting as matron of the Water Hickory Clan. How did she do?"

Wink gestured awkwardly. "Better than I'd expected. I think she genuinely understands the errors made by the former clan leaders."

Sora nodded. "She'd better."

Her voice had an edge to it that Wink had never heard before.

She changed the subject. "Rockfish was so relieved when he saw you, I thought he might faint."

Almost no expression crossed Sora's face. Her eyes tightened the slightest bit.

Wink continued, "I'm glad you're home. You have saved me from having to make a difficult decision."

"What decision?"

"I wasn't sure you were alive. And with the death of—of Long Fin"—she paused to gather her strength—"a gap opened in the government. I've been worried about whom to appoint to replace him. Now I don't have to make that decision."

Sora said, "This past half moon has been excruciating for everyone, hasn't it?"

"Especially you." Wink patted her hand and released it. "You've told me almost nothing about what happened in Eagle Flute Village, or afterward in Forbidden Village."

"I will. I just need more time to—to patch myself back together first. Then I'll tell you everything."

"It must have been terrible."

Sora blinked, and a stony expression came over her face. "Rockfish has informed me that he wishes to go back to his own people."

Wink's mouth dropped open. "Why? Did he give you any reason?"

Sora drew a spiral on her purple dress with her fingertip. "Perhaps I gave him one," she said cryptically. Then she asked, "How is Feather Dancer?"

"He's well. Why?"

"Oh, I don't know what to say to him. I'll never be able to repay him, Wink. When we were being held captive in Eagle Flute Village, he fought to protect me.

He tried to kill Flint. Other than you, he's the only person in my life who has ever truly believed in me."

Wink watched the thoughts swimming behind Sora's eyes as those eyes filled with tears. Was she thinking about the priest? Suddenly, Sora lurched forward, onto her hands and knees, and vomited on the floor.

Wink rose and ran for a bowl. She put it in Sora's hands and sank down beside her to comfortingly pat her back.

When she'd finished retching, Sora said, "Forgive me, it's been happening the past two days. Usually in the mornings. I don't know what's wrong."

Wink frowned. A single thought formed behind Sora's eyes, and Wink read it as though it were written in stone. "Sora . . . are you pregnant?"

She wiped her mouth with the back of her hand and stared at the dancing flames. Finally, she whispered, "I may be."

"But I didn't think that was possible. I thought you were—"

"So did I."

They stared at each other.

Sora had been a captive in an enemy village. She had undoubtedly been raped. Perhaps many times. Had she told Rockfish it wasn't his child? Was that the reason he wanted to go home to his own people?

Gently, Wink said, "Do you know who the father is?"

Sora exhaled hard and looked away. "Not for certain."

"Well, it doesn't matter. You know that. The child will belong to our clan. In fact . . ." *Blessed gods, this can't be happening. It's too good to be true.* "Sora, I—I thought, after the death of Long Fin, that Shadow Rock Clan was doomed to lose the rulership of the Black Falcon Nation. But if you're carrying a girl—"

"I'm not." She tenderly put a hand to her abdomen, and some of the pain in her eyes eased.

"How do you know it's not a girl?"

"I just know."

The strange statement left Wink floundering, wondering what had happened that would convince Sora the child was male. "Sora, what happened with Priest Strongheart? Please, tell me. Are you well? Did he cure you?"

Grief tightened her face, and Wink could see in her eyes that she had loved the man. Which meant the child was probably Strongheart's.

Sora said, "He told me I am cured."

It started to rain again; soft drops pattered on the roof and glistened as they fell through the smokehole onto the flames.

"Do you feel cured?"

Sora lifted a shoulder, but said, "Yes."

"What about the Midnight Fox? Is it dead?"

As though Wink wasn't meant to hear the answer, Sora murmured, "For many winters, the Midnight Fox kept a child alive inside him. It was his sole purpose. Now . . ."

When her voice trailed away, Wink asked, "What? Now, what?"

Sora took a deep breath. "I don't think the Midnight Fox is dead. I still feel it there, curled up deep inside me. But it's Dreaming. I—I catch glimpses. Sometimes."

"Glimpses?"

Sora tilted her head, as though trying to decide how to describe them. "Splinters of light falling through utter darkness . . . tears the color of jade . . . and I hear howls so beautiful they make me weep." She gazed at Wink with dark quiet eyes. "I think they're happy dreams."

Wink didn't say anything.

"I'm tired, Wink. Very, very tired."

"I'm sure you are." Wink got to her feet. "I'll go and let you sleep.

"But tomorrow, I want to hear more."

"Of course."

As Wink walked toward the door curtain, she heard Sora rise and go to her sleeping bench.

Wink walked down the corridor, toward the front entrance where Feather Dancer stood guard.

As she ducked beneath the curtain, he swiftly turned and asked, "Is the chieftess well?"

Their gazes held.

"She told me that she doesn't know what to say to you, that you are the only person in her life who has ever truly believed in her, and she'll never be able to repay you for that devotion."

His jaw clenched with emotion. He bowed his head for a long time. "She has already repaid me, Matron, by coming home. That's all I require."

Wink's lips quirked into a smile. "I suspect, in the end, she will find a way to do more, Feather Dancer."

He gave her a curious look, but Wink walked away, heading toward the steps cut into the front of the Chieftess' Mound.

In the distance, gauzy clouds clung to the tops of the trees, and she could see raindrops stippling the surface of Persimmon Lake.

As she walked out into the plaza, streaks of sunlight broke through the storm. They shone down into the plaza like the golden lances of the gods.

THE BLANKETS WERE SO WARM, THE HOUSE SO quiet, it took only heartbeats for Sora's shadow-soul to drift away from her body and begin the long agonizing walk up the Red Hill. . . .

I wrap the cleaned bones of my stillborn child in a blanket and carry him up the steep trail to the top of the Red Hill, where a ladder leans against the ramada. It's awkward, carrying the baby while climbing the ladder to the roof, but I make it, and step out onto the thatch. A scatter of bones already covers the roof.

I hug the bundle and rock back and forth, begging Skyholder to give me the strength to perform my sacred duty.

Bones clack together as I clutch the baby to my breast one last time.

When I start to unfold the blanket, a strange numbing palsy possesses my hands. My fingers won't grasp the fabric.

"Flint?" I call into the gale. "Flint, where are you?"

Nearby, dry leaves crunch underfoot, and a deep familiar voice soothes, "I've been waiting for you. I knew you'd come."

I turn to look down the trail, and the ache in my chest becomes almost unbearable. The blue light of dawn gleams from Strongheart's luminous eyes. I can't stop looking at him. He's tall and skinny, and whole. The wounds in his chest are gone.

He climbs the ladder to the roof and holds out his hands. "Let me help you."

I extend the bundle, and he takes it.

"Are you all right?" he asks as he peels back the layers of fabric.

"I miss you."

He smiles and tenderly touches my cheek. "I'm right here, Sora. I'll always be here."

As he opens the bundle, he lifts his voice in the Death Song. He places the first bone on the roof with the others, then holds out the bundle for me to take one. Together we place all the tiny white bones on the roof.

When it is done, we stand up, and Strongheart wraps his arms around me. I am aware of his body against mine, holding me up as my knees shake, of the smoky scent of his shirt. I press my face to his shoulder and weep.

"Don't cry." His hand, large but very light of touch, smooths my hair. "Everything is all right. He has a body, Sora. At last, he's safe."

I feel him lean down and kiss my hair; then he whispers in my ear. . . .

"You are both safe now."

SELECTED BIBLIOGRAPHY

Davis, Dave D. *Perspectives on Gulf Coast Prehistory.* Gainesville: University Press of Florida/Florida State Museum, 1984.

Dickens, Roy S., Jr. *Cherokee Prehistory. The Pisgah Phase in the Appalachian Summit Region.* Knoxville: University of Tennessee Press, 1981.

Gilliland, Marion Spjut. *The Material Culture of Key Marco, Florida.* Port Salerno: Florida Classics Library, 1989.

Hickerson, Harold. "The Feast of the Dead Among the Seventeenth-Century Algonkians of the Upper Great Lakes." *American Anthropologist* 62: 81–107.

Hudson, Charles. *The Southeastern Indians.* Knoxville: University of Tennessee Press, 1989.

Kilpatrick, Jack Frederick, and Anna Gritts Kilpatrick. *Notebook of a Cherokee Shaman.* Smithsonian Contributions to Anthropology, Vol. 2, Number 6. Washington, D.C.: Smithsonian Institution Press, 1970.

———. *Run Toward the Nightland. Magic of the Oklahoma Cherokees.* Dallas: Southern Methodist University, 1967.

———. *Walk in Your Soul: Love Incantations of the Oklahoma Cherokees.* Dallas: Southern Methodist University, 1965.

Lewis, Barry, and Charles Stout, eds. *Mississippian Towns and Sacred Space: Searching for an Architectural*

Grammar. Tuscaloosa: University of Alabama Press, 1998.

McEwan, Bonnie G. *Indians of the Greater Southeast: Historical Archaeology and Ethnohistory.* Gainesville: University Press of Florida, 2000.

Milanich, Jerald T. *Archaeology of Precolumbian Florida.* Gainesville: University Press of Florida, 1994.

———. *Florida Indians and the Invasion from Europe.* Gainesville: University Press of Florida, 1995.

———. *McKeithen Weeden Island: The Culture of Northern Florida, A.D. 200–900.* New York: Academic Press, 1984.

———. *The Timucua.* Oxford: Blackwell Publishers, 1996.

Milanich, Jerald T., and Charles Hudson. *Hernando de Soto and the Indians of Florida.* Gainesville: University Press of Florida, 1993.

Neitzel, Jill E. *Great Towns and Regional Polities in the Prehistoric American Southwest and Southeast.* Albuquerque: University of New Mexico Press, 1999.

Purdy, Barbara A. *The Art and Archaeology of Florida's Wetlands.* Boca Raton, Fla.: CRC Press, 1991.

Sears, William H. *Fort Center: An Archaeological Site in the Lake Okeechobee Basin.* Gainesville: University of Florida Press, 1994.

Swanton, John R. *The Indians of the Southeastern United States.* Washington, D.C.: Smithsonian Institution Press, 1987.

Trigger, Bruce G. *The Children of Aataentsic. A History of the Huron People to 1660.* Montreal: McGill-Queen's University Press, 1987.

Walthall, John A. *Prehistoric Indians of the Southeast:*

Archaeology of Alabama and the Middle South. Tuscaloosa: University of Alabama Press, 1990.

Willey, Gordon R. *Archaeology of the Florida Gulf Coast.* Gainesville: University of Florida Press, 1949.

Wrong, George M. *Sagard's Long Journey to the Huron Country.* Toronto: The Champlain Society, 1939.

The continuation of a sweeping epic set against the majesty of the great Mississippian chiefdoms

FROM *USA TODAY* BESTSELLING AUTHORS

W. Michael Gear and Kathleen O'Neal Gear

People of the Thunder

People of the Thunder continues the story of Trader, Old White, Morning Dew, and Two Petals that began in *People of the Weeping Eye*. The great empire of Cahokia has fallen, and in its shadow, numerous nations scramble to obtain power.

"The Gears have consistently captured early Native American life with precision, detail, and narrative excitement."

—*Booklist* on *People of the Moon*

www.tor-forge.com

978-0-7653-1439-0 • 0-7653-1439-8 • IN HARDCOVER JANUARY 2009